tion

INVERCLYDE LIBRARIES
CENTRAL LIBRARY
This book is to be returned on or before
the last date above. It may be borrowed
for a further period if not in demand.
Enquiries and renewals tel.: (01475) 712323

HIGHA
PORT GL

D1420198

LONGMAN

verclyde Libraries

34106 002486244

Addison Wesley Longman Limited
Edinburgh Gate, Harlow,
Essex CM20 2JE. England
and Associated Companies throughout the world.

First published in the Bridge Series 1973
by arrangement with Chatto & Windus Ltd.
This edition first published in Longman Fiction 1996

ISBN 0 582 27522 9

Set in Adobe Granjon 10.5pt
Printed in China

Acknowledgements

We are grateful to Addison Wesley Longman Limited
for permission to use in the Word List definitions
adapted from the third edition of the
Longman Dictionary of Contemporary English
© Addison Wesley Longman Limited (1995).

Cover photographs © Addison Wesley Longman Limited/Gareth Boden

Advanced level books in the Longman Fiction series are simplified with reference to the Longman
Defining Vocabulary and the British National Corpus 1990.
Vocabulary level: 3000 words

Contents

			page
Introduction			i
Chapter	1	The Centre	1
Chapter	2	State Conditioning	7
Chapter	3	Off Duty	13
Chapter	4	Bernard Marx	17
Chapter	5	The Social Sea	24
Chapter	6	Passion	32
Chapter	7	Among the Savages	41
Chapter	8	John	52
Chapter	9	My Father!	60
Chapter	10	New Lives	64
Chapter	11	Emotional Problems	70
Chapter	12	Love and Hate	74
Chapter	13	Death	79
Chapter	14	Realities	83
Chapter	15	In the Service of Happiness	89
Chapter	16	The New God	96
Chapter	17	John Alone	99
Word List			111
Activities			113

Introduction

Aldous Huxley wrote that "all literature is a mixture . . . of magic and science", and his own life contained a large measure of these two elements. He was born in 1894 in Surrey, England, into a family of brilliant scientists and educators. After a calm and happy childhood, he went to Eton College in 1908, intending eventually to study medicine. The first great upset of his life followed a little later, when his mother, to whom he was very close, died of cancer. After that, an eye disease left the young Huxley almost blind, and he was forced to abandon his plans to become a doctor.

After an operation on his eyes, and after learning Braille (a method of reading by touch, used by the blind), Huxley went to Oxford University to study English literature. During his time there he suffered another great shock when his brother Trevenen killed himself. Despite his problems, Huxley successfully finished his studies in 1916. In this same year his first book, a collection of poems, was published.

In 1919 Huxley began working as a journalist for a magazine called the *Athenaeum* and he later became the drama critic for the *Westminster Gazette*. By 1921 he was able to make a living from his other writings and no longer needed to work as a journalist. In the two years that followed, Huxley wrote a great deal and travelled widely. In Italy he became friends with the writer D. H. Lawrence. In 1937 he moved to the United States, and it was here that he developed interests in philosophies, religions and spiritual matters. He settled in California, hoping that the warmer climate would improve his eye condition, and lived there until his death from cancer in 1963.

As well as novels, of which *Crome Yellow* (1921), *Antic Hay* (1923), *Those Barren Leaves* (1925), *Point Counter Point* (1928), *Brave New World* (1932), *Eyeless in Gaza* (1936) and *Island* (1962) are the best known,

Huxley also wrote short stories, poetry, plays, critical essays and travel books.

Huxley was a young man in the 1920s and the climate of hopelessness felt by many at that time had a great effect on his work. These were the years after World War I, the most destructive war in human history, a war in which so many lives had been senselessly thrown away. It was in this war that weapons of mass destruction had been used for the first time, destroying the late nineteenth-century belief that science could bring only improvements to the quality of people's lives. The fact that science can be put to use for good and for evil is a theme to which Huxley constantly returns in his writing.

Brave New World is Huxley's most famous work. Set in an imaginary future 600 years on, it represents the author's reflections on the state of contemporary society. Huxley questioned the values of an uncertain post-war society in which people, in their search for happiness, spent their money on consumer goods and their time seeking easy sex. Huxley was writing in a period when life often seemed hopeless and high ideals rare; when thoughts about dealing with the universal problems of living together in peace seemed to be sacrificed to the pleasures of living for the moment. His perception of an urgent need for social stability and order was coupled with anxiety about current political tendencies and particularly his fear of American world domination, which seemed at the time to be increasingly likely. These issues are important to Huxley, but they are presented here in a highly readable, often humorous way. The inventiveness, excitement and energy that run through the book have made it hugely successful from the day it was published.

In *Brave New World* the author projects us into a future in which conventional values have been turned on their head. Humans are bred and conditioned by scientific methods to create a society in which people have peaceful, reasonably happy lives but no individual freedom or opportunity for passion. It is a world in which all aspects of individuality are discouraged and group unity is everything; a world in which faithfulness to one sexual partner is viewed with disapproval and in which unhappiness can be cured by a couple of *soma* tablets. When John is brought to this New World from a Reservation of social outcasts known as savages, his behaviour and attitudes throw into sharp perspective all the issues that interest Huxley so much. Should we look forward to a 'brave new world'? Or should we fear it?

Chapter 1

The Centre

A low grey building, of only thirty-four floors. Over the main entrance the words CENTRAL LONDON HATCHING AND CONDITIONING CENTRE, and below that the motto of the World State, COMMUNITY, IDENTITY, STABILITY.

The enormous room on the ground floor faced towards the north. Cold in spite of the summer outside, in spite of the high temperature of the room itself, a thin, unfriendly light came in through the windows, falling on the glass and bright metal and coldly shining white surfaces of a laboratory. The feeling of winter was strong there. The clothes which the workers wore were white, and their hands were covered with pale rubber, the colour of a dead man's face. The light was frozen and dead. Only from the shining equipment on the long work tables did it borrow a certain rich life, lying along the polished surfaces like butter.

"And this," said the Director, opening the door, "is the Fertilising Room."

Bent over their instruments, three hundred Fertilisers were working away, as the Director of Hatching and Conditioning entered the room, deep in the silence of people completely occupied by their task. A group of newly arrived students, very young, pink and inexperienced, followed nervously, rather unhappily, at the Director's heels. Each of them carried a notebook, in which, whenever the great man spoke, he wrote desperately. The occasion was an unusual one. Opportunities of hearing from the DHC for Central London about the work of the Centre were rare, but he always insisted on personally conducting his new students round the various departments.

"Just to give you a general idea," he would explain to them. For of course some general idea they must have, if they were to do their work intelligently — though as little of one as possible, if they were to be good and happy members of society. For details, as everyone knows, lead to virtue and happiness; generalities, though necessary for some purposes, are dangerous. A peaceful and efficient society is based on practical workers, not on thinkers.

"Tomorrow," he would add, with a mixture of friendliness and firmness in his manner, "you will be settling down to serious work. You won't have time for generalities. Meanwhile . . ."

Meanwhile it was a privilege. Straight from the Director's mouth into the notebook. The boys wrote their notes as fast as they could.

Tall and rather thin but upright, the Director advanced into the room. He had a long chin and big teeth which were only just covered by his full, curved lips when he was not speaking. Old, young? Thirty? Fifty? Fifty-five? It was hard to say, and anyhow, in this year of stability AF 632,* nobody thought of asking such a question.

"I shall begin at the beginning," said the DHC, and the more eager students wrote in their notebooks: *Begin at the beginning*. "This is where the process starts." And opening a door specially constructed to prevent heat from escaping he showed them shelf after shelf of numbered test tubes. "The week's supply of eggs. These are kept at blood heat, while the male fertilising agents," and here he opened another door, "have to be kept at thirty-five degrees instead of thirty-seven. Blood heat would destroy their fertilising power."

While the pencils raced over the pages of the notebooks, he gave them a brief description of the modern fertilising process; spoke first, of course, of the operation necessary for its beginning — "the operation accepted

---

*AF: a variation on the more usual AD which, in a Christian dating system, means "in the year of our Lord". The F (here and in phrases like "Our Ford", "his fordship" and "fordliness") is a reference to Henry Ford (1863–1947) who founded the first factory for the mass-production of cars. Ford has now become the god of the New World and is used instead of "lord".

willingly for the good of Society, not to mention that those on whom it is performed are paid six months' extra salary"; described how the eggs after removal from the body were kept alive and developing; mentioned the liquid in which they were kept; and leading the students to the work tables, showed how this liquid was taken from the test tubes; how, drop by drop, it was carefully examined on specially warmed slides; how the eggs were examined to make sure they were normal and then counted; how they were afterwards transferred to a container which (and he now took them to watch the operation) was placed in a warm solution in which the male fertilising agents swam freely, at least one hundred thousand of them in every thousandth of a litre of solution; how, after ten minutes, the container was lifted out of the solution; how the fertilised eggs went back on the shelves. There the Alphas and Betas* remained until definitely bottled, but the Gammas, Deltas and Epsilons were brought out again, after only thirty-six hours, to be treated by Bokanovsky's Process.

"Bokanovsky's Process," repeated the Director, and the students underlined the words in their little notebooks. "One egg, one embryo, one adult — that is normal. But a bokanovskified egg will divide into many others — from eight to ninety-six — and every one will grow into a perfectly formed embryo, and every embryo into a full-sized adult. Producing ninety-six human beings instead of one. Progress."

But one of the students was foolish enough to ask what advantage this method of producing human beings had over the natural way.

"My good boy!" The Director turned sharply and stared at him. "Can't you see? Can't you *see*? Bokanovsky's Process is one of the major instruments of social stability!"

Social stability. Standard men and women, all exactly the same. The

---

*Alpha, Beta, Gamma, Delta and Epsilon: the names of the first five Greek letters. When these letters are used as examination grades, Alpha is the highest.

staff for the whole of a small factory from one single bokanovskified egg.

"If we could bokanovskify without limit, then for the first time in history, we should truly reach our aim of Community, Identity, Stability. But unfortunately," the Director shook his head, "there is a limit to how much we *can* bokanovskify."

Ninety-six seemed to be the limit, seventy-two a good average.

Noticing a fair-haired and red-faced young man who happened to be passing, the Director called to him.

"Mr Foster. Come along with us and give these boys the benefit of your knowledge by explaining the processes the embryos go through."

Mr Foster smiled. "With pleasure." They went.

The Bottling Room was a scene of ordered activity. Pieces cut from the pigs' stomachs came up from the Organ Store below in little lifts. The lift doors flew open. The assistant had only to reach out a hand, take a piece, place it in the bottle and smooth it down, and before the bottle had travelled out of reach along the endless belt another piece had come up from below ready to be fitted into yet another bottle, the next in that slow, never-ending procession on the belt.

The bottles advanced, and the next group of assistants made a small cut in each piece of stomach as it moved past them in its container, dropped into the cut an egg taken from one of the test tubes, smoothed the edges of the cut over it, poured in the salt solution in which it was to grow . . . and already the bottle had passed into the next room. Here the date of bottling and all necessary details about its contents were marked on it.

They passed through a room where details of all the bottles were stored on cards. These details were used by the officials who had to calculate the numbers in each group needed for Society at any time. From here they sent their figures to the Fertilising Room, which must provide the embryos that they asked for.

Opening a door, Mr Foster now led the way down a stairway into a room below ground level, still very hot and with all daylight carefully shut out. The only light was artificial light, red and faint.

"Embryos are like photograph film," said Mr Foster, smiling at his own joke. "They can only stand red light."

This was where the sex and social grade of each future human being was determined. He pointed out three long rows of shelves, one above the other. Along them the bottles moved very slowly during the treatment given to them before they came out into the daylight and the contents changed from the condition of embryos into that of living people. Two hundred and sixty-seven days was the time required for the whole process to be completed. On the two hundred and sixty-seventh morning, daylight and independent existence — so-called.

"But in that time we've managed to do a lot to them," said Mr Foster with an air of satisfaction. "Oh, a very great deal."

As they walked round, he described the various methods of treatment according to the sex an embryo was to possess and the place which it was to fill in the Community. He told the students how the babies emerged from these processes already graded as Alphas or Epsilons, as future factory workers or future . . . "future World Controllers", he was going to say, but corrected himself and said "future Directors of Production" instead.

The Director smiled.

Mr Foster now became very technical in his explanations. He described how the embryos were developed in a rich solution which took the place of blood. He showed how the supply of oxygen to each grade of embryo was controlled in order to produce the correct degree of development of brain or body at each stage in its growth. He paused by a shelf of embryos who were to work in hot countries or in factories such as steel works. They passed through a chamber in which the embryos were exposed first to heat and then to an extremely unpleasant degree of cold, time after time, so that when they were ready to leave the bottles and become babies they would love heat and fear cold. Later on their minds would be trained to think what their bodies already felt. "Down here we condition them to need heat for their physical development," ended Mr Foster. "The nurses upstairs will teach them to enjoy it."

"And that," added the Director, "that is the secret of happiness and virtue — liking what you've *got* to do. All our conditioning aims at that: making people like their unavoidable place in Society."

In a space between two chambers a nurse was carrying out a very delicate operation with a needle on the contents of a passing bottle. The students and their guides stood watching her for a few moments in silence.

"Well, Lenina," said Mr Foster, when at last she took the needle from the bottle and straightened herself up.

The girl turned towards them. In spite of the faint red light, one could see that she was very pretty.

"Henry!" She smiled at him, showing a row of shining white teeth.

"What are you giving them?" asked Mr Foster, making the tone of his voice very professional.

"Oh, the usual tropical fever and sleeping sickness."

"Tropical workers start being treated at this point to resist tropical diseases," Mr Foster explained to the students. Then, turning back to Lenina, "Ten to five on the roof this afternoon," he said, "as usual."

"Wonderful," the Director smiled at Lenina, touching her bottom lightly with one hand.

He led the students to a shelf where rows of the next generation's chemical workers were being trained to survive exposure to great quantities of lead and other dangerous substances. On another shelf the first of a group of two hundred and fifty future rocket engineers had just reached a point on the moving belt at which a special machine began to spin their bottles at a regular speed. "To improve their sense of balance," Mr Foster explained. "Doing repairs on the outside of a rocket in flight is not an easy job. We reduce the supply of artificial blood when they're the right way up, so that they're hungry, and double it when they're upside down. They learn to like being turned over and over like this. In fact, they're only truly happy when they're standing on their heads."

"And now," Mr Foster went on, "I'd like to show you some very interesting conditioning for Alpha-Plus Intellectuals. We have a big group of them on Shelf 5, Middle Level."

But the Director had looked at his watch. "Ten to three," he said. "No time for the intellectual embryos, I'm afraid. We must go up to the Nurseries before the children have finished their afternoon sleep."

Chapter 2

State Conditioning

Mr Foster left them at the door of the Unbottling Room, where the embryos were taken from their bottles to go through the all-important process of passing into the condition of babies, the first real stage on their way through life as human beings. The DHC and his students took the nearest lift and were carried up to the fifth floor.

INFANT NURSERIES. CONDITIONING ROOMS, said the sign.

The Director opened a door. They were in a large empty room, very bright and sunny. The whole of the southern wall was a single window. Half a dozen nurses, wearing the official uniform of white coat and trousers, with their hair hidden under white caps, were putting out big bowls of roses in a long row across the floor.

The nurses stood still as a mark of respect when the DHC came in.

"Put out the books," he said.

In silence the nurses did as he had ordered. The books were put out between the rose bowls — a row of attractive children's books, each open at some brightly coloured picture of an animal or a fish or a bird.

"Now bring in the children."

The nurses hurried out of the room and returned in a minute or two, each pushing a set of four shelves on wheels. Each shelf, protected with wire nets, was loaded with eight-month-old babies, all exactly alike (a Bokanovsky Group, it was evident) and all (since they were Deltas) dressed in light brown clothes.

"Put them down on the floor."

The infants were unloaded.

"Now turn them round so that they can see the flowers and books."

The babies were turned round. At once they began to move towards the books, attracted by the bright colours and pretty shapes. As they moved, the sun came out from behind a passing cloud. It shone on the roses and on the pictures, lighting them up and making them even more beautiful. The babies cried out loud with pleasure and excitement.

The Director rubbed his hands with satisfaction. "Excellent," he said. "It might have been done on purpose."

Some of the babies were already at their goal. Their little hands reached out uncertainly, touching the roses and the brightly coloured pages. The Director waited till they were all happily busy. "Watch carefully," he said. And lifting his hand, he gave the signal.

The Head Nurse, who was standing at the other end of the room, pressed a switch.

There was a violent explosion. Alarm bells sounded.

The children screamed. Their faces were ugly and twisted with fear.

"And now," the Director shouted, making himself heard above the noise, "now we will make the lesson clearer with a small electric shock."

He waved his hand again and the Head Nurse pressed a second switch. The screams of the babies became desperate. Their little bodies stiffened. Their little arms and legs made sudden movements as if they were being pulled by hidden wires.

"We can send electric shocks all the way through that part of the floor," shouted the Director in explanation. "But that's enough," he signalled to the nurse.

The explosions ceased, the bells were silent, the little arms and legs stopped moving and the screams grew less desperate.

"Offer them the flowers and books again."

The nurses obeyed; but at the mere sight of the roses and of those pretty pictures of pet animals, the infants drew back in horror and began to cry louder than ever.

"Notice that," said the Director with an air of great satisfaction, "notice that."

Books and loud noises, flowers and electric shocks; already in the minds of the babies these pairs of things were connected, and repeated lessons would make the connection permanent.

"They'll grow up with what at one time would have been called a 'natural' hatred of books and flowers. They'll be safe from books and flowers all their lives." The Director turned to his nurses. "Take them away again."

Still screaming, the babies in brown were loaded on to their shelves again and wheeled out, leaving behind them the smell of sour milk and a very welcome silence.

One of the students held up his hand to ask a question. He could see quite clearly why you couldn't have low-grade people wasting the Community's time over books, and that there was always the risk of their reading something that might upset their conditioning in some way, but he couldn't understand about the flowers. Why go to the trouble of making it impossible for Deltas to like flowers?

Patiently the DHC explained. If the children were made to scream at the sight of a rose, there were good economic reasons for this. Not so very long ago (about a century) Gammas, Deltas, even Epsilons had been conditioned to like flowers in particular and wild nature in general. The idea was to make them want to be out in the country at every opportunity and so force them to use transport.

"And didn't they use transport?" asked the student.

"Quite a lot," the DHC replied. "But nothing else."

Flowers and scenery, he pointed out, have one great fault; they are free. A love of nature keeps no factories busy. It was decided to take away the love of nature, at any rate among the lower classes; to take away the love of nature, but *not* the need for transport. For of course it was necessary that they should keep on going to the country, even though they hated it. The problem was to make them use transport for a reason which was economically better than a mere affection for flowers and scenery. It was solved.

"We condition the lower classes to hate the country," ended the Director. "But at the same time we condition them to love all country sports. Then we make sure that country sports require expensive equipment. So they buy and use manufactured articles as well as transport. That is the reason for those electric shocks."

"I see," said the student, full of admiration.

"Once upon a time," the Director began speaking again, "once upon a time, while Our Ford was still on earth, there was a little boy called Reuben Rabinovitch. He was the child of Polish-speaking parents. You know what Polish is, I suppose?"

"A dead language, like French and German."

"And 'parent'?"

There was an awkward silence. Several of the boys turned red in the face. They had not yet learned the difficult art of distinguishing between immorality and pure science. One, at last, had the courage to raise a hand.

"Human beings used . . ." he paused. The blood rushed to his cheeks. "Well, they used to give birth to their own babies."

"Quite right." The Director nodded.

"And when the babies were unbottled . . ."

"'Born'," came the correction.

"Well, then they were the parents — I mean, not the babies, of course; the other ones." The boy fell silent, covered with confusion.

"In short," the Director said, "the parents were the father and mother." This was really strong language, even if it was science and not just dirty talk. The words fell with a crash into the awkward silence. "Mother," he repeated loudly, rubbing in the science. He leant back in his chair. "These," he said, "are unpleasant facts; I know it. But then most historical facts *are* unpleasant."

He returned to Little Reuben. "One night his father and mother (crash! crash!) forgot to turn off the radio in his room. (For you must remember that in those days children were brought up by their parents and not in State Conditioning Centres.) While he was asleep, a radio programme was broadcast from London. Next morning Little Reuben woke up and repeated word for word a long lecture by that strange old writer George Bernard Shaw. His (crash!) and (crash!) could not understand a word of it, of course. They thought their child had suddenly gone mad and sent for a doctor. He, fortunately, understood English, recognised the speech which he had also listened to on the previous evening, realised the importance of what had happened and sent a letter to a medical journal about it.

"The principle of sleep-teaching had been discovered," said the Director. "Now come with me."

The students followed him to another lift, from which they stepped out at the fourteenth floor.

"Silence, silence," whispered a loudspeaker. "Silence, silence," repeated other loudspeakers at intervals along the corridor. The students and even the Director himself, without thinking, obeyed the voices and walked on the tips of their toes. They were Alphas, of course, but even

Alphas have been well conditioned. "Silence, silence." The air of the fourteenth floor was heavy with the whispered command.

The Director carefully opened a door. They entered a room where the light was very low. Eighty little beds stood in a row against the wall. All that could be heard was light regular breathing and a continuous hum like the sound of very faint voices speaking softly at a great distance.

A nurse stood up as they entered.

"What's the lesson this afternoon?" the Director asked quietly.

"We had Elementary Sex for the first forty minutes," she said, "but now it's gone over to Elementary Class Consciousness."

The Director walked slowly down the long line of beds. In each one lay a child asleep. Eighty little boys and girls with pink, healthy faces lay there softly breathing. There was a whisper under every bedcover.

"Elementary Class Consciousness, did you say? Let's have it repeated a little louder by the loudspeaker."

At the end of the room a loudspeaker hung on the wall. The Director walked up to it and pressed a switch.

". . . all wear green," said a soft but very distinct voice, beginning in the middle of a sentence, "and Delta children all wear light brown. Oh no, I *don't* want to play with Delta children. And Epsilons are even worse. They're too stupid to be able to read or write. Besides, they wear black, which is such an ugly colour. I'm *so* glad I'm a Beta."

There was a pause, then the voice began again.

"Alpha children wear grey. They work much harder than we do, because they're so clever. I'm really very glad I'm a Beta, because I don't work so hard. And then we are much better than the Gammas and Deltas. Gammas are stupid. They all wear green, and Delta children all wear light brown. Oh no, I *don't* want to play with Delta children. And Epsilons are even worse."

The Director pushed back the switch. The voice sank to the faintest of whispers which could just be heard from beneath the eighty bedcovers.

"They'll have that repeated a hundred and twenty times three times a week for thirty months while they are sleeping, then they go on to a more advanced lesson. Sleep-teaching is the most powerful force of all time in social education. The child's mind becomes these suggestions and the total of these suggestions is the child's mind. And not only the child's mind. The adult's mind too, all his life long. The mind that thinks and desires and decides. But all these suggestions are our suggestions!" The Director almost shouted in his enthusiasm. "Suggestions from the State."

A noise made him turn round.

"Oh, Ford!" he said in another tone, "I've woken the children."

Chapter 3

Off Duty

In the four thousand rooms of the Centre, the four thousand electric clocks struck four. From the loudspeakers came the order:

"Main Day-shift off duty. Second Day-shift on duty. Main Day-shift off . . ."

From her dark underground room Lenina Crowne shot up seventeen floors, turned to the right as she stepped out of the lift, walked down a long passage and, opening the door marked GIRLS' DRESSING ROOM, went to a cupboard with her name on it in which her outdoor clothes were hanging. There she took off her working uniform and went along to the bathroom. Streams of hot water were running into or out of a hundred baths. The other girls who had come off duty were talking at the tops of their voices. A loudspeaker was playing a loud and cheerful military march.

After her bath, Lenina went back to her cupboard to change into her outdoor clothes.

"Hullo, Fanny," she said to the young woman who had the cupboard next to hers.

Fanny worked in the Bottling Room, and her second name was also Crowne. But as the two thousand million people of the world had only ten thousand names between them, this was not surprising.

"Who are you going out with tonight?" asked Fanny.

"Henry Foster."

"Again?" Disapproval showed on Fanny's face. "Do you mean to tell me you're *still* going out with Henry Foster?"

"Well, after all," Lenina protested, "it's only about four months since I've been having Henry."

"*Only* four months! What a thing to say! And what's more," Fanny went on, pointing an accusing finger, "there's been nobody else in all that time, has there?"

Lenina turned red, but she said loudly, "I don't see why there should have been."

"Oh, she doesn't see why there should have been," Fanny repeated, as though to an unseen listener behind Lenina's left shoulder. Then, with a sudden change of tone, "But seriously," she said, "I do think you ought to be careful. It's such bad behaviour to go on and on like this with one man. At forty, or thirty-five, it wouldn't be so bad. But at *your* age, Lenina! No, it really won't do. And you know how angry any affair makes the DHC if it goes on too long. Four months of Henry Foster, without having another man — well, he'd be very angry if he knew.

"Of course there's no need to give him up," Fanny went on in a kinder voice. "Have somebody else from time to time, that's all. He has other girls, doesn't he?"

Lenina admitted it.

"Of course he does. Trust Henry Foster to be the perfect gentleman

— always correct. And then there's the Director to think of. You know how he insists on correct behaviour."

Lenina nodded. "He touched me on the bottom this afternoon."

"There, you see!" said Fanny. "That is an example of correct manners. A model of strictly conventional behaviour."

"And to tell the truth," said Lenina, "I'm beginning to get just a bit tired of nothing but Henry every day." She pulled on her underwear. "Do you know Bernard Marx?" she asked, trying not to show too much interest by her tone of voice.

Fanny looked surprised and a little alarmed. "Bernard Marx of the Psychology Department? You don't mean to say . . . ?"

"Why not? Bernard's an Alpha-Plus. Besides, he asked me to go to one of the Savage Reservations with him. I've always wanted to see a Savage Reservation."

"But his reputation?"

"What do I care about his reputation?"

"They say he doesn't like any of the State sports."

"They say, they say," laughed Lenina.

"And then he spends most of his time by himself —*alone*." There was horror in Fanny's voice.

"Well, he won't be alone when he's with me. And anyhow, why do people behave so badly to him? I think he's rather sweet." She smiled to herself; how shy he had been! Frightened almost — as though she had been a World Controller and he a Gamma-Minus machine minder.

"But he's so ugly," said Fanny.

"But I rather like his looks."

"And then he's so *small*." Smallness was so horribly and so definitely low-grade.

"I think that's rather sweet," said Lenina. "One feels one would like to have him as a pet. You know. Like a cat."

Fanny was shocked. "They say somebody made a mistake when he was still in the bottle — thought he was a Gamma and began treatment to slow down development before the mistake was discovered. That's why he's so short."

"What nonsense!" Lenina was very angry.

Back to back, Fanny and Lenina continued their changing in silence.

"There, I'm ready," said Lenina after a while. Fanny remained silent, with her head turned away. "Let's make peace, Fanny darling. Do I look all right?" Her jacket was made of bottle-green cloth with green artificial fur at the wrists and collar. A smart green and white cap shaded her eyes. She had on a pair of green shorts, with long white socks turned down below the knee. Her shoes were bright green and highly polished. Round her waist she wore a green belt of artificial leather, filled with the official supply of contraceptives.

"Perfect!" cried Fanny with a smile. She could never resist Lenina's friendliness for long. "And what a perfectly *sweet* Malthusian belt.* I simply must get one like it."

And all this time, the shelves of bottles were moving forward with the faint humming of machinery, slowly, steadily, thirty-three centimetres an hour, in the faint light of countless red lamps.

*Thomas Malthus (1766–1834) wrote an essay in which he warned that if population is not controlled, it increases more quickly than the food and other resources needed to support it.

Chapter 4

Bernard Marx

The lift was crowded with men from the Alpha Changing Rooms, and Lenina was greeted with many nods and smiles as she stepped into it. She was a popular girl and, at one time or another, had spent a night with almost all of them.

In a corner she saw the small, thin body, and the sad face of Bernard Marx.

"Bernard!" She moved to his side. "I was looking for you." Her voice could be clearly heard above the sound of the rising lift. The others looked round. "I'd simply *love* to come with you in July," she went on. (There! She was making known publicly that she was going to stop being faithful to Henry. Fanny ought to be pleased, even though it was with Bernard.) "That is," said Lenina with her warmest smile, "if you still want to have me."

Bernard's pale face turned red. "Why?" she wondered in surprise, but at the same time touched by this strange proof of her power.

"Hadn't we better talk about it somewhere else?" he said awkwardly, looking terribly uncomfortable.

"As though I had been saying something shocking," thought Lenina. "He couldn't look more upset if I'd made a dirty joke — asked him who his mother was or something like that."

"I mean, with all these people about . . ." He was covered with confusion.

Lenina laughed out loud with honest amusement. "How funny you are!" she said; and she quite genuinely did think him funny. "You'll give me at least a week's warning, won't you?" she went on in a different voice. "I suppose we take the Blue Pacific Rocket? Does it start from the

Charing-T Tower?* Or is it from Hampstead?"

Before Bernard could answer, the lift stopped.

"Roof!" called the Epsilon-Minus liftman in his ugly voice. He opened the gates.

It was warm and sunny on the roof. The summer afternoon was filled with the hum of passing helicopters, and the deeper note of the rocket-planes speeding out of sight through the bright sky five or six miles overhead. Bernard Marx drew a deep breath. He looked up into the sky and round about him and finally down into Lenina's face.

"Isn't it beautiful?" His voice trembled a little.

She smiled at him with an expression of the most sympathetic understanding. "Simply perfect for Obstacle Golf," she answered warmly. "And now I must fly, Bernard. Henry gets cross if I keep him waiting. Let me know in good time about the date." And waving her hand she ran away across the wide flat roof towards the helicopter parks. Bernard stood watching the flash of her white legs, the sunburnt knees bending and unbending, and the soft movement of those well-fitted shorts beneath the bottle-green jacket as she ran lightly over the roof. His face wore an expression of pain.

Henry had had his machine wheeled out of its lock-up and, when Lenina arrived, was already sitting in the pilot's seat, waiting.

"Four minutes late," was all he said as she climbed in beside him. He started the engines and set the lifting blades in motion. The machine shot straight up into the air. Henry increased the speed and the sound of the blades grew higher and thinner; they were rising at almost two kilometres a minute. London grew smaller and smaller beneath them. The huge table-topped buildings became smaller and smaller. In the

---

*Charing-T Tower: T is a reference to a Model T Ford car. In the New World, T has become the religious sign instead of the Cross. Charing Cross stands outside Charing Cross railway station in London.

middle of them the tall finger of the Charing-T Tower lifted towards the sky the shining circle of its landing-platform.

Huge white clouds lay sleepily in the blue air above their heads. Out of one of them suddenly dropped a small bright-red insect.

"There's the Red Rocket," said Henry, "just come in from New York." Looking at his watch, he added, "Seven minutes behind time." He shook his head. "These Atlantic services — they're getting more and more irregular."

He reduced the speed of the lifting blades and the helicopter stopped rising; he set the forward engine in motion and they moved ahead. When the machine had enough forward speed to fly on its planes, he shut off the power from the lifting blades.

They flew over factory after factory. In one place an army of black and light brown workmen was laying a new surface on the Great West Road. At Brentford the Television Corporation's factory was like a small town.

"They must be changing the shift," said Lenina. "What a horrible colour light brown is," she added, unconsciously repeating the sleep-taught lessons of her early years. Gamma girls and the undersized Epsilons crowded round the entrances, or stood in lines to take their places in the trains. Beta-Minuses came and went among the crowd. The roof of the main building was alive with helicopters arriving and departing.

"My word," said Lenina, "I'm glad I'm not a Gamma."

Ten minutes later they had arrived at the golf course and had started their first round of Obstacle Golf.

With eyes lowered to avoid meeting the eyes of his fellow creatures, Bernard hurried across the roof. He felt worried and lonely. Even Lenina was making him suffer, although she meant well. He remembered those weeks during which he had looked and wished and almost given up hope of ever having the courage to ask her. Did he dare risk being shamed by a cruel refusal? But if she were to say yes, what joy! Well, now she had said it and he was still unhappy, unhappy that she should have thought it such a perfect afternoon for Obstacle Golf, that she should have hurried away to join Henry Foster, that she should have found him funny for not wanting to talk of their most private affairs in public. Unhappy, in a word, because she had behaved as any good, healthy English girl ought to behave and not in some other unusual, extraordinary way.

He opened the door of his lock-up and called to a couple of Delta-Minus attendants to come and push his machine out on to the roof. The helicopter park was staffed by a single Bokanovsky group, and the men were twins, small, black and very ugly. Bernard gave his orders in the sharp tone of one who does not feel certain of his authority. Bernard's height was eight centimetres short of the standard Alpha height. Contact with members of the lower classes always reminded him painfully of this fault and made him speak to them more roughly than was natural to him.

He climbed into the plane and a minute later was flying south towards the river.

The various Departments of Propaganda and the College of Emotional Engineering were housed in a single sixty-floor building in Fleet Street. On the lower floors were the presses and offices of the three great London newspapers — *The Hourly Radio*, an upper-class sheet, the pale-green *Gamma Gazette*, and, on light brown paper and in very short words, *The Delta Mirror*. Then came the Departments of Propaganda by Television and by Artificial Voice and Music — twenty-two floors of them. Above were the research laboratories and the studio rooms in which the Sound Track Writers and Artificial Music Writers did their delicate work. The top eighteen floors were occupied by the College of Emotional Engineering.

Bernard landed on the roof of Propaganda House and stepped out.

"Ring down to Mr Helmholtz Watson," he ordered the Gamma-Plus attendant, "and tell him that Mr Bernard Marx is waiting on the roof."

He sat down and lit a cigarette.

Helmholtz Watson was writing when the message came down.

"Tell him I'm coming at once," he said and replaced the receiver. Then, turning to his secretary, "I'll leave you to put my things away," he went on in the same official tone; and, taking no notice of her inviting smile, got up and walked quickly to the door.

He was a powerfully built man with a deep chest and broad shoulders, yet quick in his movements. In a masterful way he was attractive and looked, as his secretary was never tired of repeating, every centimetre an Alpha-Plus. By profession he was a lecturer at the College of Emotional Engineering (Department of Writing) and, in the intervals of his educational activities, a working Emotional Engineer. He wrote regularly for *The Hourly Radio* and had a great gift for writing mottos and easily remembered phrases.

"Able," was the opinion of those above him. "Perhaps" (and they would shake their heads and lower their voices) "a little *too* able."

Yes, a little too able. They were right. Too much intelligence had produced in Helmholtz Watson effects very like those which, in Bernard Marx, were the result of a body not sufficiently developed. Too little bone and muscle had set Bernard apart from his fellow men. That which had made Helmholtz feel so uncomfortably alone was too much ability. But although Bernard had suffered all his life from this feeling, it was only recently that Helmholtz had become aware of it. A first-class sportsman, an untiring lover, an excellent committee man and very popular socially, he had nevertheless realised quite suddenly that sport, women, professional and social activities were not, so far as he was concerned, the most important things in life. Really, deep down, he was interested in something else. But in what? That was the problem which Bernard had come to discuss with him — or rather, since it was always Helmholtz who did all the talking, to listen to his friend discussing, once again.

Three lovely girls from the Department of Propaganda by Artificial

Voice took hold of his arm as he stepped out of the lift.

"Oh, Helmholtz darling, do come and have a day out with us on Exmoor." They hung on to his arm in their efforts to persuade him.

He shook his head and pushed his way through them. "No, no."

"We're not inviting any other man."

But Helmholtz was not moved even by this pleasant promise. "No," he repeated, "I'm busy." And he walked firmly on. The girls followed him. It was not until he had actually climbed into Bernard's plane and shut the door that they gave up following him. They were offended by his refusal.

"These women!" he said as the machine rose into the air. "These women!" And he shook his head in his annoyance.

"Too awful." Bernard pretended to agree, although he silently wished that he could have as many girls as Helmholtz did, and with as little trouble. He was seized with a sudden urgent need to talk about his own success. "I'm taking Lenina Crowne to New Mexico with me," he said, trying to keep the pride out of his voice.

"Are you?" said Helmholtz with no show of interest at all. The rest of the short flight passed in silence. When they had arrived and were comfortably seated in Bernard's room, Helmholtz began to speak.

"Did you ever feel," he asked slowly, "as though you had something inside you that was only waiting for you to give it the chance to come out? Some sort of extra power that you could be using if you knew how?"

"You mean all the emotions one might be feeling if things were different?"

Helmholtz shook his head. "Not quite. I'm thinking of a strange feeling I sometimes get, a feeling that I've got something important to say and the power to say it — only I don't know what it is, and I can't make any use of the power. If there was some different way of writing . . . Or else something different to write about. I'm pretty good at inventing phrases that seem new and exciting even if they're about something completely obvious. But that doesn't seem enough. It's not enough for the phrases to be good; what you make with them ought to be good too."

"But your things *are* good, Helmholtz."

"Oh, as far as they go. But they go such a little way. They aren't important enough, somehow. I feel I could do something much more important. Yes, and more forceful, more violent. But what? What is there more important to say? Words are the most powerful of weapons if you use them properly — they'll cut through anything. But what's the good of that if the things you write about have no power in them? Can you say something about nothing? That's my problem. I try and I try . . ."

"Quiet!" said Bernard suddenly, lifting a warning finger; they listened. "I believe there's somebody at the door," he whispered.

Helmholtz got up, moved silently across the room, and with a sharp quick movement threw the door wide open. There was, of course, nobody there.

"I'm sorry," said Bernard, feeling and looking uncomfortably silly. "I suppose I've let things worry me a bit. I think people are talking about me all the time."

He passed his hand across his eyes and breathed deeply. "You don't know the trouble I've had recently," he said, almost tearfully. He was filled with a sudden wave of self-pity. "You just don't know."

Helmholtz Watson listened with a certain sense of discomfort. "Poor little Bernard," he said to himself. But at the same time he felt rather ashamed for his friend. He wished Bernard would show a little more pride.

Chapter 5

The Social Sea

By eight o'clock the light was failing. The loudspeakers in the tower of the Obstacle Golf Club House began, in a more than human voice, to announce the closing of the courses. Lenina and Henry gave up their game and walked back towards the Club.

An endless humming of helicopters filled the darkening air. Every two and a half minutes a bell and the scream of whistles announced the departure of one of the light trains which carried the lower-class golfers back from their separate course to the city.

Lenina and Henry climbed into their machine and started off. At eight hundred feet Henry slowed down the lifting blades, and they hung for a moment or two above the landscape. The forest of Burnham Beeches stretched like a great pool of darkness towards the bright shore of the western sky. Deep red at the horizon, the last of the sunset was turning through orange into yellow and a pale watery green. To the north, beyond and above the trees, a factory for the manufacture of artificial baby food shone with a fierce electric brightness from every window of its twenty floors. Beneath them lay the buildings of the Golf Club — the huge lower-class building and, on the other side of a dividing wall, the smaller houses reserved for Alpha and Beta members. The paths leading to the railway station were black with the insect-like crowds of lower-class golfers. From under the glass roof a lighted train shot out into the open. Following it with their eyes across the dark plain, their attention was drawn to the buildings of the Slough Crematorium. For the safety of night-flying planes, its four tall chimneys were lit up and topped with bright red danger signals.

"Why do the chimneys have those platforms round them?" inquired Lenina.

"To recover phosphorus from the air," explained Henry. "On their way up the chimney the gases go through four separate treatments. The phosphorus used to be lost every time they burnt a dead body. Now they recover over ninety-eight per cent of it. More than a kilo and a half per adult body. Which makes nearly six hundred thousand kilos of phosphorus every year from England alone." Henry spoke with a happy pride, as delighted at this fact as though he had been responsible for it. "Fine to think that we can go on being socially useful even after we're dead. Making plants grow."

Lenina, meanwhile, had turned her eyes away and was looking down beneath her at the railway station. "Fine," she agreed. "But odd that Alphas and Betas won't make any more plants grow than those nasty little Gammas and Deltas and Epsilons down there."

"All men are physically and chemically equal," said Henry. "Besides, even Epsilons perform valuable services."

"Even an Epsilon . . ." Lenina suddenly remembered an occasion when, as a little girl at school, she had woken up in the night and noticed, for the first time, the whispering that went on all the time when she was asleep. She saw again the beam of moonlight, the row of small white beds; heard once more the soft, soft voice that said (the words were there, never to be forgotten after being repeated so many times all through the night): "Everyone works for everyone else. We can't do without anyone. Even Epsilons are useful. We can't do without anyone . . ." Lenina remembered her first shock of fear and surprise, her doubts and questions as she lay awake for half an hour; and then, under the influence of those endless repetitions, the gradual calming of her mind, the peaceful sinking into sleep . . .

"I suppose Epsilons don't mind being Epsilons," she said out loud.

"Of course they don't. How can they? They don't know what it's like being anything else. We'd mind, of course. But then we've been differently conditioned. Besides, we are hatched from different eggs."

"I'm glad I'm not an Epsilon," said Lenina sincerely.

"And if you were an Epsilon," said Henry, "your conditioning would have made you no less thankful that you weren't a Beta or an Alpha."

He put the machine into forward motion and headed towards London. Behind them, in the west, the deep red and orange were almost gone. A dark bank of cloud had spread over the sky. As they flew over the Crematorium, the plane shot up on the column of hot air rising from the chimneys, only to fall as suddenly when it passed into the cold air beyond.

"What fun that was!" Lenina laughed.

But Henry's tone was, for a moment, almost sad. "Do you know what caused all that fun? It was some human being finally and definitely disappearing. Going up in a cloud of hot gas. It would be interesting to know who it was: a man or a woman, an Alpha or an Epsilon . . ." Then, forcing himself to sound more cheerful, "Anyhow," he concluded, "there's one thing we can be certain of; whoever he may have been, he was happy when he was alive. Everybody's happy now."

"Yes, everybody's happy now," repeated Lenina. They had heard the words over and over again, a hundred and fifty times a night for twelve years.

Every second Thursday Bernard had to attend a Unity Service. After an early dinner with Helmholtz he said goodbye to his friend and, getting into a taxi on the roof, told the man to fly to the Fordson Community Singery. The machine rose a couple of hundred metres, then headed east and, as it turned, there before Bernard's eyes, enormous and beautiful, was the Singery. Lit by powerful lamps, its three hundred and twenty metres of white artificial stone shone snow-white over Ludgate Hill. At each of the four corners of its helicopter platform a huge T stood out blood-red against the night, and from the mouths of twenty-four vast golden loudspeakers came deep artificial music.

"Oh dear, I'm late," Bernard said to himself as he first caught sight of

Big Henry,* the Singery clock. And sure enough, as he was paying off his taxi, Big Henry sounded out the hour. "Ford," sang out a vast, deep voice from all the golden loudspeakers. "Ford, Ford, Ford . . ." Nine times. Bernard ran for the lift.

The great hall for Ford's Day ceremonies and other mass Community Sings was at the bottom of the building. Above it, a hundred to each floor, were the seven thousand rooms used by Unity Groups for their services every two weeks. Bernard dropped down to floor thirty-three, hurried along the corridor, waited for a moment outside Room 3210, then, making up his mind, opened the door.

Thank Ford! He was not the last. Three chairs of the twelve arranged round the circular table were still unoccupied. He slipped into the nearest of them as silently as he could. Turning towards him, the girl on his left inquired, "What were you playing this afternoon? Obstacle or Technic?"

Bernard looked at her (Ford! it was Morgana Rothschild) and had to admit, feeling very ashamed, that he had been playing neither. Morgana stared at him in surprise. There was an awkward silence.

Then she turned away and entered into conversation with the more sporting man on her left.

"A good beginning for a Unity Service," thought Bernard unhappily. If only he had given himself time to look round instead of hurrying for the nearest chair! He could have sat between Fifi Bradlaugh and Joanna Diesel. Instead of which he had gone and blindly planted himself next to Morgana. *Morgana*! Ford! Those black eyebrows of hers — that eyebrow, rather — for they met above the nose. Ford! And on his right was Clara Deterding. True, Clara was not ugly. But she was really *too* fat. Whereas Fifi and Joanna were absolutely right. Light-haired, with good figures, not too large . . . And it was that unpleasant fellow Tom Kawaguchi who

---

*Big Henry: an imitation of the name Big Ben, the famous clock outside the Houses of Parliament, London

now took the seat between them.

The last to arrive was Sarojini Engels.

"You're late," said the President of the Group severely. "Don't let it happen again."

Sarojini apologised and slid into her place between Jim Bokanovsky and Herbert Bakunin. The group was now complete, the unity circle perfect. Man, woman, man, woman, in an unbroken ring the whole way round the table. Twelve of them waiting to be made one, to come together, to melt into each other, ready to lose their twelve separate selves in a single being.

The President stood up, made the sign of the T, and, turning on the artificial music, released the soft, continuous beating of drums and the low sweet notes of instruments that repeated and repeated the brief, familiar tune of the First Song of Unity. Again, again — the tune reached inside them, affecting not the ear, not the mind, but the heart, the soul.

The President made the sign of the T and sat down. The service had begun. The holy *soma* tablets were placed in the centre of the dinner table. The loving cup of ice-cream *soma* was passed from hand to hand and, with the sentence "I drink to my end", twelve times tasted. Then, accompanied by the artificial music, the First Song of Unity was sung.

Ford, we are twelve; oh, make us one,
Like drops within the Social Sea;
Oh, make us now together run
And in Unity forever be.

Twelve verses, full of the same deep feeling. And then the loving cup was passed a second time. All drank. Untiringly the music played. The drums beat. The Second Song of Unity was sung.

Come, Greater Being, Social Friend,
Help us with our Twelve-in-One!
We long to die, for when we end,
Our larger life has just begun.

Again twelve verses. By this time the *soma* had begun to work. Eyes and cheeks shone, happy, friendly smiles broke out on every face. Even Bernard felt a little happier. When Morgana Rothschild turned and smiled at him, he did his best to smile back. But the eyebrow, that black two-in-one, was still there; however hard he tried, he couldn't feel attracted by Morgana.

The loving cup had passed right round the table. Lifting his hand, the President gave a signal. The group began the Third Song of Unity. As verse followed verse, their voices trembled with a growing excitement. The President reached out his hand; and suddenly a Voice, a deep strong Voice, more musical than any merely human voice, richer, warmer, full of love, spoke from above their heads. Very slowly, "Oh, Ford, Ford, Ford," it sang, on a lower and quieter note each time the name was repeated. A warm feeling spread through the bodies of those who listened. Tears came into their eyes.

Then, suddenly, the voice cried out loudly, "Listen!" They listened. After a pause it went on, in a whisper which somehow was more effective than the loudest cry, "The feet of the Greater Being." Again it repeated the words: "The feet of the Greater Being." The whisper almost died. "The feet of the Greater Being are on the stairs." And once more there was silence. Among the group, the excitement grew until it was almost beyond control. The feet of the Greater Being — oh, they heard them, they heard them, coming softly down the stairs, coming nearer and nearer down the imaginary stairs. The feet of the Greater Being. And suddenly the breaking point was reached.

Her eyes staring, her lips parted, Morgana Rothschild sprang to her feet.

"I hear him," she cried. "I hear him."

"He's coming," shouted Sarojini Engels.

"Yes, he's coming, I hear him." Fifi Bradlaugh and Tom Kawaguchi rose to their feet together.

"Oh, oh, oh," cried Joanna.

"He's coming!" shouted Jim Bokanovsky.

The President leaned forward and, with a touch, let loose a fever of drum-beating.

"Oh, he's coming!" screamed Clara Deterding, as though she were having her throat cut.

Feeling that it was time for him to do something, Bernard also jumped up and shouted: "I hear him; he's coming." But it wasn't true. He heard nothing and, for him, nobody was coming. Nobody, in spite of the music, in spite of the ever-growing excitement. But he waved his arms, he shouted as loudly as any of them; and when the others began to stamp their feet and move forward, he also stamped and began to move.

Round they went, a circle of dancers, each with hands on the waist of the dancer in front, round and round, shouting all together, stamping in time to the music with their feet, beating it, beating it out on the bottoms in front; twelve pairs of hands beating as one. The sound of twelve bottoms hit at once. Twelve as one, twelve as one. "I hear him, I hear him coming." The music grew quicker; faster beat the feet, faster fell the hands on the bottoms in front. And all at once a great deep artificial voice sang out the words which announced the final act of unity, the coming of the Twelve-in-One, the return of the Greater Being. "Orgy-porgy," it sang, while the drums beat ever more wildly:

Orgy-porgy, Ford and fun,
Kiss the girls and make them one.
Boys at one with girls at peace
Orgy-porgy gives release.*

"Orgy-porgy," the dancers took up the holy words, "Orgy-porgy, Ford and fun, kiss the girls . . ." And as they sang, the lights began to go down slowly and at the same time to grow warmer, richer, redder, until at last they were dancing in the blood-red light of an Embryo Store. For a while the dancers continued to go round, stamping their feet and beating out the time of the song. "Orgy-porgy . . ." Then the circle weakened, broke, fell on the ring of soft benches which surrounded the table and the twelve chairs in an outer ring. "Orgy-porgy."

Gently, softly the deep Voice sang on.

They were standing on the roof. Big Henry had just sung eleven. The night was calm and warm.

"Wasn't it wonderful?" said Fifi Bradlaugh. "Wasn't it simply wonderful?" She looked at Bernard with shining eyes, happy, completely satisfied, at peace with the whole world.

"Yes, I thought it was wonderful," he lied and looked away. The sight of Fifi's happy face only made him feel his own separateness more keenly. He was as unhappily alone now as he had been when the service began; more alone because of his unsatisfied desire for something that he could not even describe to himself. Separate and unhappy, while the others were being united with the Greater Being; alone even in Morgana's arms — much more alone, more hopelessly himself than he had ever been in his life before. He had come out from that blood-red light into the common, cold light of the electric lamps with a feeling of hopelessness. He was terribly unhappy, and perhaps (her shining eyes accused him),

---

*Orgy-porgy: an imitation of the first words of a children's nonsense song, which in full is:

Georgie-porgie pudding and pie
Kissed the girls and made them cry,
When the boys came out to play
Georgie-porgie ran away.

An orgy is a wild party with a lot of eating, drinking and sexual activity.

perhaps it was his own fault. "Quite wonderful," he repeated; but the only thing he could think of was Morgana's eyebrow.

Chapter 6

Passion

Odd, odd, *odd*, was Lenina's opinion of Bernard Marx. So odd, indeed, that during the next few weeks she wondered more than once whether she shouldn't change her mind about the New Mexico holiday and go instead to the North Pole with another man. The trouble was that she knew the North Pole. She had been there last summer and, what was more, had found it pretty uncomfortable. Nothing to do and the hotel was terribly old-fashioned with no television in any of the bedrooms. No, certainly she couldn't face the North Pole again. And she had only been to America once before, and even then, only for a cheap weekend in New York with a man whose name she had forgotten. The idea of flying west again, and for a whole week, was very inviting. Moreover, for three days of that week they would be in the Savage Reservation. Not more than half a dozen people in the whole Centre had ever been inside a Savage Reservation. As an Alpha-Plus psychologist, Bernard was one of the few men she knew who had official permission to go there. It was the chance of a lifetime for Lenina. And yet Bernard was so odd that she had worried about taking it.

She had discussed this anxiously one night with Henry when they were in bed together. "Oh," said Henry, "poor Bernard's harmless. Some people never really learn through their conditioning what correct behaviour is. Bernard's one of them. Luckily for him, he's pretty good at his job. Otherwise the Director would never have kept him. But he's harmless, you can be sure."

Harmless perhaps, but also pretty upsetting. That unhealthy determination, to start with, to do things in private. Which meant, in practice, not doing anything at all. For what was there that one *could* do in private? (Apart, of course, from going to bed: but one couldn't do *that* all the time.) Yes, what *was* there? The first afternoon they went out together was particularly fine. Lenina had suggested a swim at a very popular bathing beach followed by dinner at the newest restaurant, which everybody went to. But Bernard thought there would be too much of a crowd. Then what about a round of Obstacle Golf? But again, no. Bernard thought that Obstacle Golf was a waste of time.

"Then what's time for?" asked Lenina in some surprise.

"For going for walks in the country. Alone with you, Lenina."

"But, Bernard, we shall be alone all night."

Bernard went red in the face and looked away. "I meant alone for talking," he said.

"Talking? But about what?" Walking and talking; that seemed a very odd way of spending an afternoon.

In the end she persuaded him, much against his will, to fly over to Amsterdam to see the Final of the Women's World Football Cup.

"In a crowd," he complained, "as usual." He remained silent and unhappy the whole afternoon; wouldn't talk to Lenina's friends, of whom they met dozens in the ice-cream *soma* bar at half time; and in spite of his unhappiness absolutely refused the chocolate *soma* ice that she bought for him to cheer him up.

"I'd rather be myself," he said. "Myself and unhappy. Not somebody else, however cheerful."

On their way back across the Channel, Bernard insisted on stopping the forward movement of his helicopter and letting it hang within a hundred feet of the waves. The weather had turned worse. A south-west wind had sprung up, the sky was cloudy.

"Look," he commanded.

"But it's horrible," said Lenina, turning her face from the window. She was frightened by the rushing emptiness of the night, by the black water rising and falling endlessly beneath them, by the pale face of the moon among the racing clouds. "Let's turn on the radio. Quick!" She reached for the switch and turned it on.

"——skies are blue inside of you," sang sixteen voices, sweet as sugar, "the weather's always——"

Then silence. Bernard had turned the radio off again.

"I want to look at the sea in peace," he said. "One can't even look with all that awful noise going on."

"But it's lovely. And I don't want to look."

"But I do," he answered. "It makes me feel as though . . ."

He stopped, searching for words with which to express himself, "As though I were more *me*, if you see what I mean. More on my own, not so completely a part of something else. Doesn't it make you feel like that, Lenina?"

But Lenina was crying. "It's horrible, horrible," she kept repeating. "After all, we're all part of something else. Everyone works for everyone else. We can't do without anyone. Even Epsilons . . ."

"Yes, I know," said Bernard bitterly. "Even Epsilons are useful! So am I. And I sometimes wish I weren't!"

Lenina was shocked by these words. "Bernard!" she said, her eyes filled with tears. "How can you think such things?"

"How can I?" he repeated, deep in thought. "No. The real problem is: How is it that I can't, or rather — because I know quite well why I can't — what would it be like if I could, if I were free — not a slave to my conditioning?"

"But, Bernard, you're saying the most awful things."

"Don't you wish you were free, Lenina?"

"I don't know what you mean. I am free. Free to have the most wonderful time. Everybody's happy nowadays."

He laughed. "Yes. 'Everybody's happy nowadays.' We begin giving the children that at five. But wouldn't you like to be free to be happy in some other way, Lenina? In your own way, for example; not in everybody else's way."

"I don't know what you mean," she repeated. Then, turning to him, "Oh, do let's go back, Bernard," she begged. "I do so hate it here."

"Don't you like being with me?"

"Yes, of course, Bernard! But this place is horrible."

"I thought we'd be more . . . more *together* here, with nothing but the sea and moon. More together than in a crowd, or even in my rooms. Don't you understand that?"

"I don't understand anything," she said firmly, "least of all why you don't take *soma* when you have these terrible ideas. You'd forget all about them. And instead of feeling unhappy, you'd be cheerful."

He looked at her in silence. "All right then," he said at last in a small, tired voice, "we'll go back." He made the machine rise sharply into the sky, then put it into forward movement. They flew in silence for a minute or two. Then, suddenly, Bernard began to laugh. Rather oddly, Lenina thought; but still, it was laughter.

"Feeling better?" she asked shyly.

For answer he lifted one hand from the controls and slipped his arm round her waist.

"Thank Ford," she said to herself, "he's all right again."

Half an hour later they were back in his rooms. Bernard swallowed four tablets of *soma*, turned on the radio and television and began to undress.

"Well," Lenina asked with a smile when they met next afternoon on the roof, "did you think it was fun yesterday?" Bernard nodded. They climbed into the plane, and off they went.

"Everybody says I have a nice body," said Lenina, stroking her own legs.

"Very nice." But there was an expression of pain in Bernard's eyes. "Like meat," he was thinking.

"But you don't think I'm too fat, do you?" She looked up anxiously. He shook his head and thought again, "Like so much meat."

"You think I'm all right?" Another nod. "In every way?"

"Perfect," he said to her. And thought to himself, "She thinks of herself that way. She doesn't mind being meat."

Lenina smiled with satisfaction. But she was happy too soon.

"All the same," he went on, after a little pause, "I still rather wish it had ended differently."

"Differently?" Were there other endings?

"I didn't want it to end with our going to bed," he said.

Lenina looked at him in surprise.

"Not at once, not the first day."

"But then what?"

He began to talk a lot of dangerous nonsense that she could hardly understand.

"I want to know what passion is," he said. "I want to feel something strongly. We are all grown-up intellectually and during working hours," he went on, "but we are infants where feeling and desire are concerned."

"Our Ford loved infants."

Bernard went on as though she hadn't spoken. "It suddenly struck me the other day that it might be possible to be an adult all the time."

"I don't understand." Lenina's tone was firm.

"I know you don't. And that's why we went to bed together yesterday — like infants — instead of being grown-up and waiting."

"But it was fun," Lenina insisted. "Wasn't it?"

"Oh, the greatest fun," he answered, but in a voice so sad, with an expression so thoroughly unhappy, that Lenina wondered if perhaps he had found her too fat after all.

"I told you so," was all that Fanny said when Lenina told her all this. "Somebody *did* make a mistake when he was in his bottle."

"All the same," Lenina insisted, "I do like him. He has such awfully nice hands. And the way he moves his shoulders — that's very attractive. But I wish he weren't so odd."

Pausing for a moment outside the door of the Director's room, Bernard drew a deep breath and prepared to meet the dislike and disapproval which he was certain of finding inside.

"A permit for you to sign, Director," he said as coolly as possible, and laid the paper on the writing table.

The Director looked at him rather angrily. But the stamp of the World Controller's office was at the head of the paper and the signature of the World Controller, Mustapha Mond, across the bottom. Everything was perfectly in order. The Director could not refuse. He wrote his initials under it in pencil and was about to give back the paper without comment when his eye was caught by something written in the body of the permit.

"For the New Mexican Reservation?" he said, and his tone, the face he lifted to Bernard, expressed a kind of worried surprise.

Surprised by his surprise, Bernard nodded. There was a silence.

The Director leaned back in his chair, deep in thought.

"How long ago was it?" he said, speaking more to himself than to Bernard. "Twenty years, I suppose. Nearer twenty-five. I must have been your age . . ." He shook his head.

Bernard felt extremely uncomfortable. He wondered what the Director would say next.

"I had the same idea as you," the Director went on. "Wanted to have a look at the savages. Got a permit for New Mexico and went there for my summer holiday. With the girl I was having at the moment. She was a Beta-Minus, and I think" (he shut his eyes), "I think she had yellow hair. Anyhow, she had a lovely body, a particularly lovely body. I remember that. Well, we went there, and we looked at the savages, and we rode about on horses and all that. And then — it was almost the last day of my holiday, then . . . well, she got lost. We'd gone riding up one of those horrible mountains, and it was terribly hot, without any wind, and after lunch we went to sleep. Or at least I did. She must have gone for a walk, alone. Whatever she did do, when I woke up she wasn't there. And the most terrible thunderstorm I've ever seen was just bursting on us. And it poured and crashed and flashed. And the horses broke loose and ran away. And I fell down, trying to catch them, and hurt my knee, so that I could hardly walk. Still I searched, and I shouted and I searched. But there was no sign of her. Then I thought she must have gone back to the rest house by herself. So I went down into the valley by the way we had come.

"My knee was very painful, and I'd lost my *soma*. It took me hours. I didn't get back to the rest house till after midnight. And she wasn't there; she wasn't there," the Director repeated. There was a silence. "Well," he went on at last, "the next day there was a search. But we couldn't find her. She must have fallen down a crack in the rocks somewhere, or been eaten by a mountain lion. Ford knows. Anyhow it was horrible. It upset me very much at the time. More than it ought to have done."

"You must have had a terrible shock," said Bernard.

At the sound of his voice the Director looked sharply at him and handed him the permit. Angry with himself at having told Bernard this secret from his past, he directed his anger at Bernard. "And I should like to take this opportunity, Mr Marx," he went on, "of saying that I'm not at all pleased with reports of your behaviour outside working hours. You may say that this is not my business. But it is. I have the good name of the Centre to think of. My workers must be beyond criticism, particularly those of the highest classes. And so, Mr Marx, I give you fair warning. If

I ever have any complaint again about your failure to submit to our rules for social behaviour, I shall ask for you to be moved to a Sub-Centre, perhaps to Iceland. Good morning." And turning away, he picked up his pen and began to write.

"That'll teach him," he said to himself. But he was mistaken. For Bernard left the room with a joyful feeling that he stood alone against the whole of the social order, with the sense of his individual importance. He was not even frightened by the Director's threats. He felt strong enough to resist severe treatment, strong enough to face even Iceland. And in any case he didn't believe that he would be called upon to face anything at all. People weren't moved for things like that. Iceland was just a threat. Walking along the passage, he actually whistled.

The journey was quite uneventful. The Blue Pacific Rocket was two and a half minutes early at New Orleans, lost four minutes in a storm over Texas, but then flew into a favourable air current and was able to land at Santa Fé less than forty seconds behind the official time.

"Forty seconds on a six and a half hour flight. Not so bad," said Lenina.

They slept that night at Santa Fé. Lenina found all the comforts that she could have wished for.

"There won't be anything like this in the Reservation," Bernard warned her. "No television, no hot water even. You mustn't come to the Reservation unless you really want to."

"But I do want to."

"Very well, then," said Bernard.

Their permit required the signature of the Director of the Reservation, to whose office they went next morning. He was full of useless information and unasked-for good advice. Once started, he went on and on in the same loud, boring voice.

". . . five hundred and sixty thousand square kilometres, divided into four distinct Sub-reservations, each surrounded by an electric fence. There is no escape. Those who are born in the Reservation — and remember, dear young lady, that in the Reservation children still are born, yes, actually born, disgusting though that may seem — must spend their whole lives there and die there. There are about sixty thousand Indians and people of mixed blood . . . absolute savages . . . our inspectors occasionally visit . . . otherwise, no contact with the civilised world . . . still preserve their shameful habits and customs . . . marriage if you know what that is, my dear young lady; families . . . no conditioning . . . Christianity and awful old belief systems like that . . . dead languages such as Spanish . . . savage wild animals . . . infectious diseases . . . priests . . . poisonous snakes . . ."

They got away at last. A message was sent to them at the hotel that, on the Director's orders, a Reservation Guard had come round with a plane and was waiting on the roof. They went up at once.

They took their seats in the plane and set off. Ten minutes later they were crossing the border that separated civilisation from savagery. Uphill and down, across the deserts of salt or sand, through forests, down into deep valleys, over wide plains and tall mountain tops, the fence marched on and on. And at its foot, here and there, a pattern of white bones, a body on the ground, marked the place where a wild animal had gone too close to the deadly wires.

"They never learn," said the pilot, pointing down at the bones on the ground below them. "And they never will learn," he said, laughing as if at a joke.

Bernard, having taken two grams of *soma*, went to sleep and woke at last to find the machine standing on the ground, Lenina carrying the suitcases into a small square house, and the pilot talking in some language that he could not understand with a young Indian.

"Malpais," explained the pilot, as Bernard stepped out. "This is the rest house. And there's a dance this afternoon at the village. He'll take you there." He pointed to the young savage, who appeared unwilling. "It'll be funny, I expect. Everything they do is funny." And with that he climbed into the plane and started up the engines. "Back tomorrow. And remember," he added for Lenina's benefit, "they're perfectly all right. Savages won't do you any harm. They've got enough experience of gas bombs to know that they mustn't play tricks." Still laughing, he moved the controls, rose into the air and was gone.

Chapter 7

Among the Savages

The flat-topped rock rose up from the yellow, dusty plain of a valley through which ran a river between high, steep banks. On the top of this rock was the Indian village of Malpais. Block above block, each storey smaller than the one below, the tall houses rose in great stone steps into the blue sky. At their feet lay an untidy group of low buildings, and on three sides the tall rocks fell straight down into the plain. A few columns of smoke rose into the still air and were lost.

"Strange," said Lenina. "Very strange." That was what she called anything that did not please her. "I don't like it. And I don't like that man." She pointed to the Indian guide who had been appointed to take them up to the village. He clearly did not like them either; even the back of the man, as he walked along, seemed to express his hatred of them.

"Besides," she lowered her voice, "he smells."

Bernard did not attempt to deny it. They walked on.

Suddenly it seemed as though the whole air had come alive and was beating, beating with the tireless movement of blood. Up there, in

Malpais, the drums were being beaten. Their feet began to obey the beat of that mysterious heart. They walked more quickly. Their path led them to the foot of the rock. Its sides rose above them like a great tower, three hundred feet to the top.

"I wish we could have brought the plane," said Lenina, looking up with dislike at the blank rock face. "I hate walking. And you feel so small when you're on the ground at the bottom of a hill."

They walked along for a time in the shadow of the rock, turned a corner and there, in a dry channel worn away by the water in former times, was the way up. They climbed. It was a very steep path that went from side to side of the channel. Sometimes the drums were almost silent, at others they seemed to be beating only just round the corner.

When they were halfway up, a large bird flew past so close to them that they felt the cold wind from his wings on their faces. In a crack in the rock lay a pile of bones. It was all frighteningly strange, and the Indian smelt stronger and stronger. They emerged at last from the channel into the full sunlight. The top of the rock was a flat platform of stone.

"Like the Charing-T Tower," said Lenina, comforting herself with the memory of something familiar and safe. But she was not allowed to enjoy this comforting comparison for long. The sound of soft footsteps made them turn round. Naked from throat to waist, their dark brown bodies painted with white lines ("like clay tennis courts" Lenina was later to explain), their faces wild, not human, painted red, black and yellow, two Indians came running along the path. Fox fur and pieces of red cloth and birds' feathers were twisted into their black hair. Great brightly coloured headdresses rose above their faces. With every step they took their silver jewellery shook and the bones and coloured stones in their necklaces knocked against each other. They came on without a word, running quietly in their animal-skin shoes. One of them was holding a feather brush. The other carried, in each hand, what looked at a distance like three or four pieces of thick rope. One of the ropes moved and twisted, and suddenly Lenina saw that they were snakes.

The men came nearer and nearer. Their dark eyes looked at her, but without the smallest sign that they had seen her or were aware of her existence. The twisting snake hung still again with the rest. The men passed.

"I don't like it," Lenina said. "I don't like it."

She liked even less what she found at the entrance to the village, where their guide had left them while he went inside for instructions. The dirt, to start with — the piles of rubbish, the dust, the dogs, the flies. Her face showed how disgusting she found it. She held her hand to her nose.

"But how can they live like this?" she cried, hardly able to believe her own eyes.

"They've been doing it for the last five or six thousand years," said Bernard, "so I suppose they must be used to it by now."

"But cleanliness is next to fordliness," she insisted.

"Yes, and civilisation is sterilisation," Bernard went on with a little smile. "But these people have never heard of Our Ford, and they aren't civilised. So there's no point in——"

"Oh!" She held his arm. "Look."

An almost naked Indian was very slowly climbing down the ladder from the first floor of one of the houses, with the trembling carefulness of extreme old age. His face was deeply lined and black. The toothless mouth had fallen in. At the corners of the lips and on each side of the chin a few long hairs shone almost white against the dark skin. The long untidy hair hung down in grey threads around his face. His body was bent, nothing but skin and bone. Very slowly he came down, pausing at each step before he placed a foot carefully on the one below.

"What's the matter with him?" whispered Lenina. Her eyes were wide with horror and shock.

"He's old, that's all," Bernard answered as carelessly as he could. He too was shocked, but he made an effort to seem unmoved.

"Old?" she repeated. "But the Director's old. Lots of people are old. They're not like that."

"That's because we don't allow them to be like that. We preserve them from diseases. We keep their bodies in good condition by scientific treatment. We give them young blood at regular intervals. We keep their body systems working perfectly. So of course they don't look like that. Partly," he added, "because most of them die long before they reach this old creature's age. Youth almost perfectly preserved till sixty, and then, crack! the end."

But Lenina was not listening. She was watching the old man. Slowly, slowly he came down. His feet touched the ground. He turned. His deep-sunken eyes were still extraordinarily bright. They looked at her for a long moment without expression, without surprise, as though she had not been there at all. Then, slowly, with bent back, the old man walked painfully past them and was gone.

"But it's terrible," Lenina whispered. "It's awful. We ought not to have come here." She felt in her pocket for her *soma* only to discover that by some mistake she had left the bottle down at the rest house. Bernard's pockets were also empty.

Lenina was left to face the horrors of Malpais unaided. They came crowding in on her. The sight of two young women giving their breasts to their babies made her redden and turn away her face. She had never seen anything so shocking in all her life. And what made it worse was that, instead of pretending to take no notice of it, Bernard kept on making open remarks about this disgustingly animal scene. He went out of his way to show how strong and individual he was.

At this moment their guide came back and, making a sign to them to follow, led the way down a narrow street between the houses. A dead dog was lying on a rubbish pile; a woman with a badly swollen neck was combing the dirt from the hair of a small girl. Their guide stopped at the foot of a ladder, then pointed upwards and forwards. They obeyed the sign — climbed the ladder and walked through a doorway at the top into a long, narrow room, rather dark and smelling of cooked fat and dirty clothes. At the further end of the room was another doorway, through which came a beam of sunlight and the noise, very loud and close, of the drums.

They went through the door and found themselves outside again. Below them, shut in by the tall houses, was the village square, crowded with Indians. Bright cloths, and feathers in black hair, and jewels and dark skins shining in the sun. Lenina put her hand to her nose. In the open space in the centre of the square were two circular platforms of bricks and beaten clay — the roofs, it was clear, of underground chambers; for in the centre of each platform was an open lid, with a ladder coming up from the lower darkness. A sound of pipe-playing came up from below and was almost lost in the steady beat of the drums.

Lenina liked the drums. Shutting her eyes, she listened to their soft repeated thunder; but she opened them again at a sudden burst of singing — hundreds of male voices crying out loudly together. A few long notes and silence, then the women's answer, thin and high. Then again the drums; and once more the deep, savage cries of the men.

Suddenly there came up from those round underground chambers a frightening band of strange beings. Wearing ugly masks or with faces painted so that they looked like nothing human, they circled in a strange dance round the square. Round and round again, singing as they went, round and round — each time a little faster; and the beat of the drums grew quicker, so that it was like fevered blood in the ears, and the crowd began to sing with the dancers, louder and louder; and first one woman screamed, and then another and another, as though they were being killed; and then suddenly the leader of the dancers left the circle, ran to a big wooden chest which was standing at one end of the square, raised the lid and pulled out a pair of black snakes. A great cry went up from the crowd, and all the other dancers ran towards him with their hands stretched out. He threw the snakes to those who arrived first, then put his hands into the chest and drew out more. And then the dance began again, to a different beat. Round they went with their snakes, twisting and turning their bodies as if they were snakes themselves. Round and round. Then the leader gave a signal and, one after the other, all the snakes were thrown down in the middle of the square. An old man came up from underground and scattered seeds over them, and from the other chamber came a woman and threw water over them from a black bottle. Then the old man lifted his hand and, suddenly, there was absolute silence. The drums stopped beating, life seemed to have come to an end. The old man pointed to the two entrances to the lower world. And slowly, raised by hands from below, there came up from the one a painted image of a large bird, from the other that of a man, naked and nailed to a cross. The old man struck his left hand with his right. Naked except for a white cotton cloth round his waist, a boy of about eighteen stepped out of the crowd and stood before him, his hands crossed over his chest, his head bent forward. The old man made the sign of the cross over him and turned away. Slowly the boy began to walk round the twisting pile of snakes. From among the dancers a tall man, wearing the mask of a mountain lion and holding in his hand a leather whip, advanced towards him. The boy moved on as though he had not noticed the other's existence. The lion-man raised his whip; there was a long pause, then a quick movement, then the whistle of the whip through the air and the loud, flat sound of the blow falling on flesh. The boy's body trembled, but he made no sound; he walked on at the same slow, steady pace. The whip struck again, again; and at every blow at first a low cry and then a deep · shout went up from the crowd. The boy walked on. Twice, three times, four times he went round the pile of snakes. The blood was streaming. Five times round, six times round. Suddenly Lenina covered her face with her hands and began to cry. "Oh, stop them, stop them," she begged.

But the whip fell and fell without pity. Seven times round. Then suddenly the boy fell forward on to his face, still without a sound. Bending over him, the old man touched his back with a long white feather, held it up for a moment, red with blood, for the people to see, then shook it three times over the snakes. A few drops fell, and suddenly the drums broke out again in a river of hurrying notes. There was a great shout. The dancers rushed forward, picked up the snakes and ran out of the square. Men, women, children, all the crowd ran after them. A minute later the square was empty, only the boy remained, flat on his face where he had fallen, quite still. Three old women came out of one of the houses, and with some difficulty lifted him and carried him in. The bird and the man on the cross kept guard for a little while over the empty square. Then, as though they had seen enough, sank slowly down below the ground, out of sight, into the lower world.

Lenina was still crying. "Too awful," she kept repeating. "Too awful! That blood." She trembled violently. "Oh, I wish I had my *soma*."

There was the sound of feet in the inner room.

Lenina sat without moving, her face buried in her hands. Only Bernard turned round.

The dress of the young man who now came towards them was Indian; but his hair was yellow, his eyes a pale blue, and his skin a white skin, although sunburnt.

"Hullo. Good day," said the stranger, in correct but odd English. "You're civilised, aren't you? You come from the Other Place, outside the Reservation?"

"Who on earth . . . ?" Bernard began in surprise.

The young man shook his head. "A most unhappy gentleman."* And pointing to the blood in the centre of the square, "Do you see that?" he

---

*A most unhappy gentleman: the Savage speaks in the style of Shakespeare. Here "unhappy" means unlucky.

asked in a voice that trembled with emotion.

"Oh, I wish I had my *soma*," cried Lenina from behind her hands.

"I ought to have been there," the young man went on. "Why wouldn't they let me be the sacrifice? I'd have gone round ten times, twelve, fifteen. Palowhtiwa only got as far as seven. They could have had twice as much blood from me. Enough to turn the seas red." He threw his arms out wide, then let them fall again in hopelessness. "But they won't let me. They dislike me for the colour of my skin. It's always been like that. Always." Tears stood in the young man's eyes. He was ashamed and turned away.

The shock made Lenina forget all about her *soma*. She took her hands away from her face and, for the first time, looked at the stranger. "Do you mean to say that you wanted to be hit with that whip?"

The young man nodded. "For the sake of the village — to make the rain come and the corn grow. And to please Pookong and Jesus. And then to show that I can bear pain without crying out. Yes," and his voice suddenly grew firmer, he turned to her lifting his head proudly, "to show that I'm a man. Oh!" he drew in his breath sharply and was silent, staring. He had seen, for the first time in his life, the face of a girl whose cheeks were not the colour of chocolate or dog-skin, whose hair was golden and beautiful, and who looked at him kindly (something he was not used to). Lenina was smiling at him; such a nice-looking boy, she was thinking, and a really beautiful body. The blood rushed up into the young man's face. He dropped his eyes, raised them again for a moment only to find her still smiling at him, and was so full of new, strange feelings that he had to turn away and pretend to be looking very hard at something on the other side of the square.

Bernard broke in with a number of questions. Who? How? When? Keeping his eyes fixed on Bernard's face (for his desire to see Lenina smiling was so strong that he simply dared not look at her) the young man tried to explain himself. Linda and he — Linda was his mother (the word made Lenina look uncomfortable) — were strangers in the Reservation. Linda had come from the Other Place long ago, before he was born, with a man who was his father. (Bernard listened eagerly.) She had gone walking alone in those mountains over there to the north, had fallen down a steep place and hurt her head. ("Go on, go on," said Bernard excitedly.) Some hunters from Malpais had found her and brought her to the village. As for the man who was his father, Linda had never seen him again. His name was Tomakin. (Yes, "Thomas" was the DHC's first name.) He must have flown away, back to the Other Place, away without her — a bad, unkind, unnatural man.

"And so I was born in Malpais," he ended. "In Malpais." And he shook his head.

The ugliness of that little house on the edge of the village!

A space of dust and rubbish separated it from the village. Two hungry dogs were pushing their noses hungrily into the rubbish at its door. Inside, when they entered, the air smelt strongly and it was loud with flies.

"Linda!" the young man called.

From the inner room a woman's voice said thickly, "Coming."

They waited. In bowls on the floor were the remains of a meal, perhaps of several meals.

The door opened. A very large yellow-haired woman came in and stood staring at the strangers, her mouth wide open in surprise. Lenina noticed with horror that two of the front teeth were missing. And the colour of the ones that remained . . . She could hardly look. So fat. And the loose, hanging cheeks, all rough and purple. And all the lines in her face and the blood marks on her nose and in her eyes. And that neck — that neck! And the cloth she wore over her head — torn and dirty. And under the brown cloth that she wore over her body, those enormous breasts, the great round stomach. Oh, much worse than the old man, much worse! And suddenly the creature burst into a flood of speech, rushed at her with her arms stretched out and — Ford! Ford! It was too horrible, in another moment she'd be sick — held Lenina tightly to her fat body and began to kiss her. Ford! Such wet kisses, and she smelt too horrible, obviously never had a bath. And she had been drinking some very strong alcohol. Lenina broke free as quickly as she could.

A twisted face stared at her. The creature was crying. "Oh, my dear, my dear, if you only knew how glad — after all these years! A civilised face. Yes, and civilised clothes. Because I thought I should never see a piece of real artificial silk again. And those lovely shorts! Do you know, dear, I've still got my old clothes, the ones I came in, put away in a box. I'll show them to you afterwards. Though, of course, the cloth has all gone into holes. I suppose John has told you what I had to suffer — and not a gram of *soma* to be had. Only a drink of *mescal* every now and then, when Popé used to bring it. Popé is a boy I used to know. But it makes you feel so bad afterwards, the *mescal* does, and sick; besides, it always made that awful feeling of being ashamed much worse the next day. And I *was* so ashamed. Just think of it, me — a Beta — having a baby; put yourself in my place!" (The mere suggestion made Lenina tremble.) "Though it wasn't my fault, I swear. I still don't know how it happened. Because I did all that I was supposed to. But all the same it happened."

She drew a deep breath, shook her head, opened her eyes again, then blew her nose on her fingers and wiped them on her skirt. "Oh, I'm so sorry," she said, seeing Lenina's look of disgust, "I oughtn't to have done that. But what *are* you to do here?" Linda shook her head. "I tried to tell them about disease and about keeping things clean when I first came here, but they didn't understand. And in the end I suppose I got used to it. And anyhow, how *can* you keep things clean when there isn't any running hot water. And look at these clothes. This horrible wool isn't like artificial material. It never wears out. It lasts and lasts, and you're supposed to mend it if it gets torn. But I'm a Beta. I worked in the Fertilising Room. Nobody ever taught me to do anything like that. It wasn't my business. Besides, it never used to be right to mend clothes. Throw them away when they've got holes in them and buy new. 'The more stitches, the less riches.' But it's all different here. It's like living with mad people. Everything they do is mad."

She lowered her voice, "Take the way they have one another here. Mad, I tell you, absolutely mad. Everyone belongs to everyone else, don't they," she whispered, pulling at Lenina's arm. Lenina nodded and turned her head away from the smell of Linda's breath. "Well, here," the other went on, "nobody's supposed to belong to more than one person. If you have people in the ordinary way, the others think you're bad. Once a lot of women came and shouted at me because their men came to see me. Well, why not? And then they rushed at me . . . No, it was too awful. I can't tell you about it." Linda covered her face with her hands and cried. "They're so hateful here, the women. Mad, mad and cruel. And of course they don't know anything about bottles or contraceptives. So they're having children all the time — like dogs. It's too disgusting. And to think that I . . . oh, Ford, Ford, Ford! And yet John *was* a great comfort to me. I don't know what I should have done without him. Even though he did get so upset whenever a man . . . Quite as a tiny boy, even. Once (but that was when he was bigger) he tried to kill poor Waihusiwa — or was it Popé? — just because I used to have them sometimes. Because I never *could* make him understand that that's what civilised people ought to do. Being mad's catching, I believe. Anyhow, John seems to have caught it from the Indians. Because, of course, he was with them a lot. Even though they were so unkind to him and wouldn't let him do all the things the other boys did. Which was a good thing in a way, because it made it easier for me to condition him a little. Though you've no idea how difficult that is. There's so much one doesn't know. It wasn't my business to know. I mean, when a child asks you how a helicopter works or who made the world — well, what are you to answer if you're a Beta and have always worked in the Fertilising Room? What are you to answer?"

Chapter 8

John

Outside, in the dust and among the rubbish (there were four dogs now) Bernard and John were walking slowly up and down.

"So hard for me to realise," Bernard was saying, "to put it all together. As though we were living in different worlds, in different centuries. A mother, and all this dirt, and gods, and old age, and disease . . ." He shook his head. "It's almost unbelievable. I shall never understand unless you explain."

"Explain what?"

"This." He pointed to the village. "That." And it was the little house outside the village. "Everything. All your life."

"But what is there to say?"

"From the beginning. As far back as you can remember."

"As far back as I can remember." John thought deeply. There was a long silence.

It was very hot. They had eaten a lot of bread and vegetables. Linda said, "Come and lie down, Baby." They lay down together in the big bed. "Sing," and Linda sang, nursery songs. Her voice grew fainter and fainter . . .

There was a loud noise, and he woke suddenly. A man was standing by the bed, enormous, frightening. He was saying something to Linda, and Linda was laughing. She had pulled the bedclothes up to her chin, but the man pulled them down again. His hair was like two black ropes, and round his arm was a lovely silver band with blue stones in it. He liked the band, but all the same he was frightened; he hid his face against Linda's body. Linda put her hand on him and he felt safer. In those other words he did not understand so well, she said to the man, "Not with John here." But the man took hold of one of his arms, and it hurt. He screamed. The man put out his other hand and lifted him up. Linda held him, saying "No, no." The man said something short and angry. He kicked and struggled; but the man carried him across to the door, opened it, put him down on the floor in the middle of the other room, and went away, shutting the door behind him. He got up, he ran to the door. Standing on the tips of his toes he could just reach the big wooden handle. He turned it and pushed; but the door wouldn't open. "Linda," he shouted. She didn't answer.

He remembered a huge room, rather dark; and there were big wooden things with strings tied to them, and lots of women standing round them — making cloth, Linda said. Linda told him to sit in the corner with the other children, while she went and helped the women. He played with the little boys for a long time. Suddenly people started talking very loudly, and there were the women pushing Linda away, and Linda was crying. She went to the door and he ran after her. He asked her why they were angry. "Because I broke something," she said. And then she got angry too. "How should I know how to do their stupid weaving?" she said. "Horrible savages." He asked her what savages were. When they got back to their house, Popé was waiting at the door, and he came in with them. He had a big bottle full of stuff that looked like water; but it wasn't water, it was something with a bad smell that burnt your mouth and made you cough. Linda drank some and Popé drank some, and then Linda laughed a lot and talked very loudly; and then she and Popé went into the other room. When Popé went away, he went into the room. Linda was in bed and so fast asleep that he couldn't wake her.

Popé used to come often. He said the stuff in the bottle was called *mescal*; but Linda said it ought to be called *soma*, only it made you feel ill afterwards. He hated Popé. He hated them all — all the men who came to see Linda. One afternoon, when he had been playing with the other children — it was cold, he remembered, and there was snow on the mountains — he came back to the house and heard angry voices in the bedroom. They were women's voices, and they said words he didn't understand; but he knew they were bad words. Then suddenly, crash! something fell over; he heard people moving about quickly, and there was another crash and then a noise of someone being hit; then Linda screamed, "Oh, don't, don't, don't!" He ran in. There were three women in dark clothes. Linda was on the bed. One of the women was holding her wrists. Another was lying across her legs, so that she couldn't kick. The third was hitting her with a whip. Once, twice, three times, and each time Linda screamed. Crying, he caught hold of the woman's brown hand and bit it as hard as he could. She cried out, pulled her hand free and gave him such a push that he fell down. While he was lying on the ground she hit him three times with the whip. It hurt more than anything he had ever felt — like fire.

"But why did they want to hurt you, Linda?" he asked that night.

"I don't know. How should I know? They say those men are *their* men." And she burst into tears.

He pressed against her. He put his arm round her neck. Linda cried out. "Oh! be careful. My shoulder. Oh!" and she pushed him away, hard. His head knocked against the wall, painfully. "Stupid boy!" she shouted; and then, suddenly, she began to hit him.

"Linda," he cried out. "Oh, mother, don't!"

"I'm not your mother. I won't be your mother. Turned into a savage," she shouted. "Having young ones like an animal . . . If I hadn't had you, I might have gone to the Inspector. I might have got away. But not with a baby. That would have been too shameful."

He saw that she was going to hit him again, and lifted his arm to protect his face. "Oh don't, Linda, please don't."

He shut his eyes, expecting the blow, but she didn't hit him. After a little time, he opened his eyes and saw that she was looking at him. He tried to smile at her. Suddenly she put her arms round him and kissed him again and again.

The happiest times were when she told him about the Other Place — how you could go flying whenever you liked, and how you could have music out of a box, and about the other boxes where you could see and hear what was happening at the other side of the world, and babies in lovely clean bottles — everything so clean, no smells and no dirt at all — and people never lonely, but living together and being happy all the time.

Sometimes, when he and the other children were tired with too much playing, one of the old men of the village would tell them strange stories of the gods and of the beginning of the world. Strange stories that he did not fully understand. Lying in bed later he would think of Heaven and London and rows of clean bottles and Jesus and Linda flying up and the great Director of World Production and Our Ford himself.

The boys said bad things about Linda and about the men who came to see her. Sometimes they laughed at him for being such a mess. When he tore his clothes, Linda did not know how to mend them. In the Other Place, she told him, people threw away clothes with holes in them and got new ones. But Linda taught him to read, drawing pictures and letters on the wall with the point of a burnt stick; and when the other boys shouted at him, he said to himself, "But I can read, and they can't. They don't even know what reading is."

When he could read well enough, Linda gave him a thin little book that she had kept in a box with her clothes from the Other Place. It was a book of instructions for Beta Embryo-Store workers, telling them what chemicals to use for various processes in the treatment of the bottled embryos. Soon he could read all the words quite well. Even the longest. But what did they mean? He asked Linda; but even when she could answer, it didn't seem to make it very clear. And generally she couldn't answer at all.

"What are chemicals?" he would ask.

"Oh, different kinds of salts for making bones develop, and solutions for keeping the Deltas and Epsilons small and unintelligent, and all that sort of thing."

"But how do you make chemicals, Linda? Where do they come from?"

"Well, I don't know. You get them out of bottles. And when the bottles are empty, you send up to the Chemical Store for more. It's the Chemical Store people who make them, I suppose. Or else they send to the factory for them. I don't know. I never did any chemistry. My job was with the embryos."

It was the same with everything else he asked about. Linda never seemed to know. The old men of the village had much more definite answers about how the world began.

One day (John thought it must have been soon after his twelfth birthday) he came home and found a book that he had never seen before lying on the floor in the bedroom. It was a thick book and looked very old. The binding had been eaten by mice. Some of its pages were loose or torn. He picked it up and looked at the title page. The book was called *The Complete Works of William Shakespeare*.

Linda was lying on the bed, drinking that horrible-smelling *mescal* out of a cup. "Popé brought the book," she said. "He found it in an old chest in the corner of the temple of the gods. It's supposed to have been there for hundreds of years. I expect it's true, because I looked at it and it seemed to be full of nonsense. Uncivilised. Still, it'll be good enough for you to practise your reading on," she continued in a thick, drunken voice. She took a last drop, set the cup down on the floor beside the bed, turned over on her side and fell into a deep sleep.

He began to read. The strange words rolled through his mind, like talking thunder. Like the drums at the summer dances, if the drums could have spoken. Like the men singing the Corn Song, beautiful,

beautiful, so that you cried; like old Mitsima saying magic over his feathers and his sticks and his bits of bone and stone — but better than Mitsima's magic, because it talked to *him*. He could only half-understand the words, but they were full of a beautiful and terrible magic.

When he was fifteen, Mitsima taught him the art of making water pots. His first pot was so badly made that it leaned over to one side. "But the next one will be better," he said to himself and began to shape another piece of clay. He learned to love the work. He found an extraordinary pleasure in making things with his hands and in learning every time to do them better. They worked all day, side by side on the river bank, singing as they sat there making pots.

"Next winter," said old Mitsima, "I will teach you to make a bow."

When boys reached sixteen, at the time of the full moon, they would go into the temple, where secrets were told to them, and they would come out men. At last it was the day when he should go in his turn. The sun went down, the moon rose. He went with the others. Men were standing, dark shapes, at the entrance to the temple. A ladder went down into a big opening below, where a red light shone. Already the leading boys had begun to climb down. Suddenly one of the men stepped forward, caught him by the arm, and pulled him out. He broke free and ran back to his place among the others. This time the man struck him, pulled his hair. "Not for you, white hair!" "Not for the son of the she-dog," said one of the other men. The boys laughed. "Go!" And as he still waited, standing on the edge of the group, "Go!" the men shouted again. One of them bent down, took a stone, threw it. "Go, go, go!" There was a shower of stones. Bleeding, he ran away into the darkness. From the red-lit hole in the ground came the sound of singing. The last of the boys had climbed down the ladder. He was alone.

All alone, outside the village, on the empty plain. The rock looked like white bones in the moonlight. Down in the valley wild dogs cried at the moon. His body hurt, the cuts were still bleeding, but it was not for pain that he cried. It was because he was all alone, because he had been driven out, into this empty world of stone and moonlight. At the edge of a high rock he sat down. The moon was behind him; he looked down into the black shadow, into the black shadow of death. He had only to take one step, one little jump . . . He held out his right hand in the moonlight. From the cut on his wrist the blood was still flowing gently. Every few seconds a drop fell, dark, almost colourless in the dead light. Drop, drop, drop. Tomorrow and tomorrow and tomorrow . . .*

He had discovered Time and Death and God.

"Alone, always alone," the young man was saying.

The words awoke a sad memory in Bernard. Alone, alone . . . "So am I," he said in a sudden desire to share his feelings with someone else. "Terribly alone."

"Are you?" John look surprised. "I thought that in the Other Place . . . I mean, Linda always said that nobody was ever alone there."

Bernard reddened uncomfortably. "You see," he said almost in a whisper, turning his eyes aside in shame, "I'm rather different from most people, I suppose. If something happens to one's treatment and one comes out of the bottle different . . ."

"Yes, that's just it." The young man nodded. "If one's different, one's certain to be lonely. They're very cruel to one. Do you know, they shut me out of absolutely everything? When the other boys were sent out to spend the night on the mountains — you know, when you have to dream which your holy animal is — they wouldn't let me go with the others. They wouldn't tell me any of the secrets. I did it by myself, though," he added. "Didn't eat anything for five days and then went out alone into those

*Tomorrow and tomorrow and tomorrow: from Shakespeare's play *Macbeth*

mountains there." He pointed.

Bernard smiled a little smile of pity at his ignorance and simplicity. "And did you dream of anything?" he asked.

The other nodded. "But I mustn't tell you what."

They fell silent for a while, then Bernard said, "I wonder if you'd like to come back to London," taking the first step in a plan which he had decided to carry out ever since, in the little house, he had realised who the "father" of this young savage must be. "Would you like that?"

The young man's face lit up. "Do you really mean it?"

"Of course. If I can get permission from the World Controller, that is."

"Linda too?"

"Well . . ." He paused doubtfully. That horrible creature! No, it was impossible. Unless, unless . . . It suddenly occurred to Bernard that her very ugliness might be enormously useful. "But of course!" he cried, making up for his first uncertainty with a show of great pleasure.

The young man drew a deep breath. "How amazing that it's coming true — what I've dreamt of all my life. Do you remember what Miranda says?"

"Who's Miranda?"

His eyes shone and his face was full of bright colour. "You know, Shakespeare's Miranda. She says how beautiful the world is . . . and the people in it." The colour suddenly grew deeper; he was thinking of Lenina — of a heavenly creature in bottle-green clothes, shining with youth and skin food, beautifully rounded in shape, sweetly smiling. "O brave new world,"* he began, then suddenly stopped and turned pale. "Are you married to her?" he asked.

"Am I what?"

"Married. You know — for ever. They say 'for ever' in the Indian words. It can't be broken."

*O brave new world: words spoken by Miranda in Shakespeare's play *The Tempest*

"Ford, no!" Bernard couldn't help laughing.

John also laughed, but for another reason — he laughed for pure joy.

"O brave new world," he repeated. "O brave new world that has such people in it. Let's start at once."

"You have the strangest way of talking sometimes," said Bernard, staring at the young man in surprise. "And, anyhow, hadn't you better wait till you actually see the new world?"

Chapter 9

My Father!

The hands of all the four thousand electric clocks in the Bloomsbury Centre's four thousand rooms marked twenty-seven minutes past two. The Centre was full of activity. Everyone was busy, everything went on in an orderly manner. The moving rows of bottles, each with its developing embryo, followed one another slowly but surely through all the stages of treatment and out into the Unbottling Room, where the newly-unbottled babies gave their first cry of horror and shock.

The sound of well-oiled machinery rose softly from below, the lifts rushed up and down. On all the eleven floors of the Nurseries it was feeding time. From eighteen hundred bottles eighteen hundred carefully labelled infants were sucking down their bottles of artificial milk.

Above them, in ten floors of Sleeping Rooms, the little boys and girls who were still young enough to need an afternoon sleep were as busy as anyone else, although they did not know it, listening to the lessons in their sleep-teaching programme. Above these again were the Play Rooms where, the weather having turned to rain, nine hundred older children were amusing themselves with bricks, sand and clay.

The girls sang happily at their test tubes, Heads of departments whistled as they worked, and from the Unbottling Room came the sound of jokes and laughter. But the Director's face, as he entered the Fertilising Room with Henry Foster, was severe.

"A public example," he was saying. "In this room, because it contains more high-class workers than any other in the Centre. I have told him to come here at half past two. Ah! Here he comes."

Bernard had entered and was approaching between the rows of tables with a manner which only just hid the fear that he felt. The voice in which he said, "Good morning, Director," was much too loud. When he tried to correct his mistake and went on to say, "You asked me to come and speak to you here," it was far too soft, a silly little whisper.

"Yes, Mr Marx," said the Director coldly. "I did ask you to come to me here. You returned from your holiday last night, I understand."

"Yes," Bernard answered.

"Yes," repeated the Director. Then, suddenly raising his voice, "Ladies and gentlemen," he cried, "ladies and gentlemen."

The girls stopped singing and raised their heads from the rows of test tubes. There was a deep silence. Everyone looked round.

"Ladies and gentlemen," the Director cried once more, "excuse me for interrupting your labours. A painful duty forces me to do so. The security of Society is in danger. Yes, in danger, ladies and gentlemen. This man — " He pointed an accusing finger at Bernard. "This man who stands before you here, this Alpha-Plus to whom so much has been given and from whom, therefore, so much must be expected, has failed to honour the trust which had been placed in him. By his sinful views on sport and *soma*, by his shameful avoidance of convention in his sex life, by his refusal to obey the teachings of Our Ford and behave out of office hours 'like a baby in a bottle," (here the Director made the sign of the T) "he has proved himself an enemy of Society, a danger, ladies and gentlemen, to all Law and Order, a man sworn to destroy Civilisation itself. For this reason I propose to dismiss him from the post he has held in this Centre. I propose immediately to apply for him to be removed to a Sub-Centre of the lowest order and, so that his punishment may be in the best interests of Society, as far as possible from any important Centre of population. In Iceland he will have small opportunity to lead others into crime by his unfordly example." The Director paused. Then, folding his arms, he turned gravely to Bernard. "Marx," he said, "can you give any reason why the judgment passed on you should not now be carried out?"

"Yes, I can," said Bernard in a very loud voice.

Somewhat surprised, "Then show it," said the Director.

"Certainly. But it's in the passage. One moment." Bernard hurried to the door and threw it open. "Come in," he commanded, and the reason came in and showed itself.

There was a cry of horror and shock. A young girl screamed. Standing on a chair to get a better view, someone upset two test tubes and their contents. Fat, loose in figure, a strange and frightening image of middle age among those firm, youthful bodies, those smooth, healthy faces, Linda came into the room, smiling a smile which twisted her features and showed her black, broken teeth. Bernard walked beside her.

"There he is," he said, pointing to the Director.

"Did you think I didn't recognise him?" Linda asked angrily. Then, turning to the Director, "Of course I knew you, Tomakin. I should have known you anywhere, among a thousand. But perhaps you've forgotten. Don't you remember, Tomakin? Your Linda." She stood looking at him, her head on one side, but with a smile that began to disappear as she saw the look of horror on the Director's face. "Don't you remember, Tomakin?" she repeated in a voice that trembled. Her eyes were anxious, alarmed. The discoloured face took on an expression of extreme grief. "Tomakin!" She held out her arms. Someone began to laugh.

"What's the meaning," began the Director, "of this criminal . . ."

"Tomakin!" She ran forward, threw her arms round his neck, hid her face on his chest.

A great shout of laughter went up.

". . . this criminal attempt at a practical joke?" the Director shouted.

Red in the face, he tried to pull himself away from her arms. She held on to him desperately. "But I'm Linda, I'm Linda." The laughter drowned her voice. "You made me have a baby," she screamed above the noise. There was an immediate and awful silence. Everyone stood there uncomfortably, not knowing where to look. The Director went suddenly pale, stopped struggling and stood, his hands on her wrists, staring down at her in horror. "Yes, a baby — and I was its mother." She broke away from him, ashamed, ashamed, and covered her face with her hands, crying. "It wasn't my fault, Tomakin. Because I always followed the instructions, didn't I? Didn't I? Always . . . I don't know how. If you knew how awful, Tomakin . . . But he was a comfort to me, all the same." Turning towards the door, "John!" she called. "John!"

He came in at once, paused for a moment just inside the door, looked round, then moved quickly across the room, fell on his knees in front of the Director, and said in a clear voice, "My father!"

The word (for *father,* unlike the really shameful word *mother,* was sometimes heard in slightly shocking jokes) put an end to the silence that had greeted his entrance. Laughter broke, burst after burst, as though it would never stop. My father — and it was the Director! My *father*! Oh Ford, oh Ford! That was really too funny! The shouts of laughter broke out again, tears streamed down the faces of those looking on. Six more test tubes were upset. My *father*!

Pale, wild-eyed, the Director stared about him, ashamed, helpless.

"My *father*!" The laughter, which had shown signs of dying away, broke out again more loudly than ever. He put his hands over his ears and rushed out of the room.

Chapter 10

New Lives

After the scene in the Fertilising Room, all upper-class London was anxious to see this funny creature who had fallen on his knees before the Director of Hatching and Conditioning — or rather the ex-Director, for the poor man had resigned immediately afterwards and never set foot inside the Centre again — had fallen on his knees and called him (the joke was almost too good to be true!) "my father". Linda, on the other hand, was of no interest at all to them. Nobody had the smallest desire to see Linda. To say one was a mother — that was no joke, it was disgusting. Moreover, she wasn't a real savage. She had come out of a bottle and been conditioned like anyone else, so she couldn't have any unusual ideas. Lastly — and this was by far the strongest reason for people's not wanting to see poor Linda — there was her appearance. Fat, having lost her youth, with a discoloured skin, bad teeth and that figure (Ford!) — you simply couldn't look at her without feeling sick, yes, really sick. So the best people were quite determined *not* to see Linda. And Linda, for her part, had no desire to see them. The return to civilisation was for her the return to *soma*, the possibility of lying in bed and taking holiday after holiday, without ever having to come back to a headache or sickness, without ever being made to feel as you always felt after *mescal*, as though you'd done something so shameful that you could never hold up your head again. *Soma* played none of these unpleasant tricks. The holiday it gave was perfect, and if waking up from it was unpleasant, it was so not in itself but only by comparison with the joys of the holiday. The answer was to make the holiday continuous. She demanded larger and more frequent amounts of *soma*. Dr Shaw was at first unwilling, then he let her have what she wanted. She took as much as twenty grams a day, many times more than the usual quantity.

"Which will finish her off in a month or two," the doctor told Bernard in confidence. "One day she will just stop breathing. Finished. And a good thing too. We can't make her young again. Nothing to be done."

Surprisingly, as everyone thought (for on a *soma*-holiday Linda was most conveniently out of the way), John objected to this treatment.

"But aren't you shortening her life by giving her so much?"

"In one sense, yes," Dr Shaw admitted. "But in another we're actually lengthening it."

The young man stared at him questioningly.

"*Soma* may make you lose a few years in time," the doctor went on. "But think of the enormous periods it can give you out of time. And as she hasn't got any serious work to do . . ."

"All the same," John argued, "I don't believe it's right."

The doctor waved his hand impatiently. "Well, of course, if you'd rather have her crying and shouting for it all the time . . ."

In the end John was forced to give in. Linda got her *soma*. From then on she remained in her little room on the thirty-seventh floor of Bernard's apartment house, with the radio and television on and the *soma* tablets within reach of her hand.

It was John, then, that they all wanted to meet. And as it was only through Bernard that John could be seen, Bernard became popular for the first time in his life. Everybody tried to get invitations to his evening parties to meet the Savage, and, as he told his friend Helmholtz Watson, he could have as many girls as he liked just for the favour of asking them round to his apartment.

"Lighter than air," said Bernard, pointing upwards.

In the sky, high, high above them, the Weather Department's balloon shone pink in the sunshine.

". . . the Savage," so said Bernard's instructions, "is to be shown civilised life in all its aspects . . ."

He was being shown a bird's-eye view of it at present, a bird's-eye view from the platform of the Charing-T Tower. The Station Master and the station's Chief Weather Expert were acting as guides. But it was Bernard who did most of the talking. Filled with his new importance, he was behaving as though, at the very least, he were a visiting World Controller. Lighter than air.

The Bombay Green Rocket dropped out of the sky. The passengers stepped out of the machine. Eight dark-skinned twins in light brown looked out of the eight windows — the stewards.

"Twelve hundred and fifty kilometres an hour," said the Station Master proudly. "What do you think of that, Mr Savage?"

John thought it very nice. "Still," he said, "Ariel could fly round the earth in forty minutes."*

"The Savage," wrote Bernard in his report to Mustapha Mond, "shows little surprise for or admiration of civilised inventions. This is partly due, no doubt, to the fact that he has heard them talked about by the woman Linda, his m—"

(Mustapha Mond made a face. "Does the silly man think I should be shocked by the word written out in full?")

"His interest is centred on what he calls 'the soul', which he regards as something entirely independent of the body, although, as I tried to point out to him . . ."

The Controller glanced quickly over the next sentences and was just about to turn the page in search of something more definite and more interesting, when his eye was caught by a series of quite extraordinary phrases . . .

". . . though I must admit," he read, "that I agree with the Savage in

---

*Ariel: a character from Shakespeare's play *The Tempest*. In fact it is Puck from *A Midsummer Night's Dream* who offers to fly round the earth in forty minutes.

finding civilised infantility too easy or, as he puts it, not expensive enough; and I would like to take this opportunity of drawing your fordship's attention to . . ."

Mustapha Mond's anger gave place almost at once to amusement. The idea of this creature trying to teach him — *him* — about the social order was really too ridiculous. The man must have gone mad. "I ought to give him a lesson," he said to himself, and laughed out loud. The lesson would be given later.

"The Savage," wrote Bernard, "refuses to take *soma*, and seems very upset because the woman Linda, his m— remains permanently on holiday. It is worth noting that, in spite of the weak mental state of his m— and the extreme ugliness of her appearance, the Savage frequently goes to see her and appears to be much attached to her — an interesting example of the way in which early conditioning can be made to change and even run against natural responses (in this case, the natural response to draw back from an unpleasant object)."

Lenina came singing into the Changing Room.

"You seem very pleased with yourself," said Fanny.

"I am pleased," she answered. "Bernard telephoned half an hour ago. He has an unexpected engagement and he asked me to take the Savage to the cinema this evening. I must hurry." She ran off towards the bathroom.

"She's a lucky girl," said Fanny to herself as she watched Lenina go.

Sunk in their deep, comfortable armchairs, Lenina and the Savage listened to the music of the electric organ. Soon the lights went down and the film began, with the figures on the screen in lifelike colours but many times larger than life-size.

The story of the film was extremely simple. It was called *Three Weeks in a Helicopter*. A young black man fell out of a helicopter on to his head, went mad, and lost control of his feelings. He developed a passion for a lovely golden-haired young Beta-Plus girl. She refused to listen to him or to have anything to do with him. He seized her and, in spite of her struggles, threw her into his helicopter and flew up with her into the sky where he kept her for three weeks, trying to make her give in to his passion. Finally, after a whole series of adventures including some exciting scenes in the air, three good-looking young Alphas succeeded in saving her. The black man was sent off to a Reconditioning Centre and the film ended in a proper and conventional manner, with the Beta girl going to bed with all her three heroes one after the other. The picture died away, the lights came on and the music filled the cinema again. It was the end of the performance.

But for Lenina it was not quite the end. As they moved slowly along with the crowd towards the lifts she still felt emotions that the film had woken in her. Her cheeks were red, her eyes were bright and she breathed deeply. She caught hold of the Savage's arm and pressed it against her side. He looked down at her for a moment, pale, pained, desiring and ashamed of his desire. He was not good enough, not . . . Their eyes for a moment met. What wonders hers promised! Passion shone in them. He looked away quickly, freed his arm from her hold. He was frightened by a feeling that he could not fully understand. He felt somehow that she might cease to be someone that he could look up to as being too good for him, and he did not want this to happen.

"I don't think you ought to see things like that," he said.

"Like what, John?"

"Like that horrible film."

"Horrible?" Lenina was very surprised. "But I thought it was lovely."

"It was shameful," he said angrily, "it was disgusting."

She shook her head. "I don't know what you mean." Why was he always so strange? Why did he always go and spoil things?

In the taxicopter he hardly looked at her. Bound by strong promises that had never been spoken, obedient to laws that had long since ceased to have any force, he sat in silence, with his head turned away from her.

The taxicopter landed on the roof of Lenina's apartment house. "At last," she thought joyfully as she stepped out. At last — even though he *had* been so strange just now. Standing under a lamp, she looked into her hand-mirror. At last. Yes, her nose *did* need powdering. She shook the loose powder from her powder case. While he was paying the taximan there would just be time. She rubbed at the shine on her nose, thinking, "He's very good-looking. No need for him to be shy like Bernard. And yet . . . Any other man would have done it long ago. Well, now at last." The bit of her face that she could see in the little round mirror suddenly smiled at her.

"Good night," said a voice behind her in a whisper full of fear. Lenina turned round sharply. He was standing inside the door of the taxicopter, his eyes fixed, staring. He had evidently been staring all this time while she was powdering her nose, waiting — but what for? Trying to make up his mind, and all the time thinking, thinking — she could not imagine what extraordinary thoughts. "Good night, Lenina," he repeated, and made a strange, desperate effort to smile.

"But, John . . . I thought you were . . . I mean, aren't you . . . ?"

He shut the door and bent down to say something to the driver. The machine rose quickly into the air.

Looking down through the window in the floor, the Savage could see Lenina's upturned face, pale in the light of the lamps. Her mouth was open, she was calling. Her figure rushed away from him. The square of the roof grew smaller and smaller as it fell away below him into the darkness.

Five minutes later he was back in his room. From its hiding place he took out his old, worn book and, carefully turning its torn and discoloured pages, he began to read *Othello*. Othello, he remembered, was like the main character of *Three Weeks in a Helicopter* — a black man.

Drying her eyes, Lenina walked across the roof to the lift. On her way down to the twenty-seventh floor she pulled out her *soma* bottle. One gram, she decided, would not be enough. Her unpleasant experience had been more than one-gram suffering. But if she took two grams she ran the risk of not waking up in time tomorrow morning. She decided to avoid both extremes, and into the hollow of her left hand she shook three half-gram tablets of *soma*.

Chapter 11

Emotional Problems

Bernard had to shout through the locked door. The Savage would not open.

"But everybody's there, waiting for you."

"Let them wait," came back the voice faintly through the door.

"But you know quite well, John, that I asked them on purpose to meet you."

"You ought to have asked me first whether I wanted to meet *them*."

"But you always came before, John."

"Yes, and that's exactly why I don't want to come again."

Bernard tried persuasion — not an easy thing to do when you have to shout through a locked door. "Just to please me. Won't you come to please me?"

"No."

"Do you seriously mean it?"

"Yes."

"But what shall I do?" cried Bernard helplessly.

"Go to hell!" shouted the angry voice from inside.

All Bernard's attempts to get John to come out failed. In the end he had to go back to his rooms and tell all the guests who were waiting there impatiently that the Savage would not be appearing that evening. They were very angry. They felt that they had been tricked into behaving politely to this unimportant little fellow Bernard Marx with the doubtful reputation and the anti-social opinions.

Lenina alone said nothing. Pale, her blue eyes filled with an unusual sadness, she sat in a corner, separated from those around her by an emotion which they did not share. She had come to the party filled with a strange feeling, a mixture of anxiety and joy. "In a few minutes," she had said to herself as she entered the room, "I shall be seeing him, talking to him, telling him" (for she had come with her mind made up) "that I like him — more than anybody I've ever known. And then perhaps he'll say . . ." What would he say? The blood rushed to her cheeks. "Why was he so strange the other night, after the cinema? So odd. And yet I'm absolutely sure he does rather like me. I'm sure . . ."

It was at this moment that Bernard had made his statement. The Savage wasn't coming to the party.

Lenina was filled with a terrible feeling of disappointment and emptiness. Her heart seemed to stop beating.

"Perhaps it's because he doesn't like me," she said to herself. And at once this possibility grew in her mind into a certainty. John had refused to come because he didn't like her. He didn't like her.

All around her the other guests were angrily discussing the Savage's refusal to meet them and blaming Bernard for all that had gone wrong. Very soon they took their leave, one after the other.

Lenina, the last to go, walked sadly out of the room. Bernard was left there all alone. Overcome with unhappiness and disappointment he dropped into a chair and, covering his face with his hands, he began to cry.

Upstairs in his room the Savage was reading *Romeo and Juliet*.

Next morning Bernard could not hide from the Savage how unhappy he felt. The Savage showed himself sympathetic, an attitude that Bernard had not expected. "You're more like what you were at Malpais," he said when Bernard had told him all his sorrows. "Do you remember when we first talked together? Outside the little house. You're like what you were then."

"Because I am unhappy again. That's why."

"Well, I'd rather be unhappy than have the false, lying happiness that you were having here."

"I'm surprised at you, saying that," said Bernard bitterly, "when it's you who were the cause of it all. Refusing to come to my party and turning them all against me!" He knew that what he was saying was unjust. He admitted to himself the truth of all that the Savage now said about the worthlessness of friends who could be turned by such slight causes into cruel enemies. But Bernard continued to feel a secret anger with the Savage in spite of the real affection that he had for him.

Bernard's other friend was Helmholtz Watson, suffering like himself because of his individual, non-conditioned ideas. Helmholtz had been officially warned that some verses that he had written and read out to a class of students at the College of Emotional Engineering were dangerous and must not be repeated. The verses were in praise of silence, of the state of being alone and able to enjoy one's own thoughts and feelings. The students had reported him to the Principal. "I'm not surprised," said Bernard. "It's quite against all their sleep-teaching. Remember, they've had at least a quarter of a million warnings against wanting to be alone."

"I know. But I thought I'd like to see what the effect would be."

"Well, you've seen now."

Helmholtz laughed. "I feel," he said after a silence, "as though I were just beginning to have something to write about. As though I were just beginning to use that secret power that I've got inside me. Something seems to be coming to me." In spite of all his troubles he seemed, Bernard thought, deeply happy.

Helmholtz and the Savage formed a liking for each other at once.

Helmholtz read out the verses that had caused him to be warned by the Principal. The Savage replied by reading some lines from his old book that excited Helmholtz as he had never been excited before in his life; but Helmholtz simply could not understand the story of *Romeo and Juliet* when John read out the play to him with deep emotion (seeing himself all the time as Romeo and Lenina as Juliet). Helmholtz shouted with laughter at the idea of a father and mother (disgusting words anyway) forcing the daughter to have someone she didn't want! And the stupid girl not saying that she was having someone else whom (for the moment, at any rate) she preferred. The situation was so dirty and at the same time so funny that Helmholtz laughed till the tears ran down his face in streams. The Savage looked at him angrily, closed his book, got up from his chair and locked it away in its drawer.

"And yet," said Helmholtz when, having got back breath enough to apologise, he managed to persuade the Savage to listen to his explanations, "I know quite well that one needs mad, impossible situations like that. One can't write really well about anything else. Why was the old fellow such a wonderful propaganda writer? Because he had so many really strong feelings, so many strange ideas to get excited about. You've got to be hurt and upset. Otherwise you can't think of the really good phrases, those that strike at the mind and the heart and live in the memory. But fathers and mothers! You can't expect me to be serious about fathers and mothers. And who's going to get excited about a boy having a girl or not having her?" (The Savage looked offended, but Helmholtz, who was looking thoughtfully at the door, saw nothing.) "No," he decided, "it won't do. We need some other kind of madness, some other kind of emotion to take possession of our minds and become the master of our imagination. But what? Where can I find it?" He was silent. Then, shaking his head, "I don't know," he said at last, "I don't know."

Chapter 12

Love and Hate

Henry Foster appeared at Lenina's side in the faint red light of the Embryo Store. "Like to come to the cinema this evening?"

Lenina shook her head without speaking.

"Going out with someone else?" It interested him to know which of his friends was being had by which other. "Is it Bernard?" he asked.

She shook her head again.

Henry noticed how tired she looked, even in that weak light.

"You're not feeling ill, are you?" he asked, in a rather worried voice, afraid that she might be suffering from one of the few remaining diseases.

Once more Lenina shook her head.

"Anyhow you ought to go and see the doctor," said Henry. "A doctor a day keeps all worries away," he added cheerfully, using a phrase that rarely failed to cheer people up.

"Oh, for Ford's sake," said Lenina, breaking her silence at last, "Shut up!" And she turned back to her workbench.

"A doctor, indeed!" She would have laughed, if she hadn't been on the point of crying. No doctor could cure what was the matter with her. She sighed deeply. "John," she whispered to herself, "John . . ."

An hour later, in the Changing Room, Fanny was protesting loudly. "But it's silly to let yourself get into a state like this. Very silly," she repeated. "And what about? A man — *one* man."

"But he's the one I want."

"As though there weren't millions of other men in the world."

"But I don't want them."

"How can you know till you've tried?"

"I have tried."

"But how many?" asked Fanny. "One? Two?"

"Dozens. But it wasn't any good."

"Well, you must keep on trying," said Fanny.

"But meanwhile . . ."

"Don't think of him."

"I can't help it."

"Take *soma*, then."

"I do."

"Well, go on taking it."

"But in the intervals I still like him. I shall always like him."

"Well, if that's the case," said Fanny with decision, "Why don't you just go and take him? Whether he wants it or no."

"But he's so strange!"

"All the more reason for being firm."

"It's all very well to *say* that."

"Don't let him go on being so silly. Act!" said Fanny. "Yes, act at once. Do it now."

"I daren't," said Lenina.

"Well, you've only got to take half a gram of *soma* first. And now I'm going to have my bath." She marched off towards the bathroom.

The bell rang. The Savage, who was impatiently waiting for Helmholtz to come so that he could tell him how he felt about Lenina, jumped up and ran to the door.

"I guessed it was you, Helmholtz," he shouted as he opened it.

There in the entrance, in a white artificial cotton sailor suit, and with a round white cap at a most attractive angle on her head, stood Lenina.

"Oh!" said the Savage, as though someone had struck him a heavy blow.

Half a gram had been enough to make Lenina forget her fears. "Hello, John," she said, smiling, and walked past him into the room.

He closed the door and followed her. Lenina sat down. There was a long silence.

"You don't seem very glad to see me, John," she said at last.

"Not glad?" cried the Savage with deep feeling. Then he suddenly fell on his knees before her, took her hand and kissed it. "I love you more than anything else in the world."

"Then why on earth didn't you say so before?" And suddenly her arms were round his neck. He felt her soft lips against his own.

"You silly boy!" she was saying. "I wanted you so much. Sweet, sweet — and if you wanted me too, why didn't you?"

In that moment he found himself thinking of the kisses in *Three Weeks in a Helicopter* that he had found so shameless. Horror, horror, horror . . . He tried to free himself. Lenina took her arms away and stood up. He thought for a moment that she had understood how he felt. But he soon realised how mistaken he was, for in a moment Lenina had taken off her sailor suit. With nothing on but her shoes and socks and her smart white cap, which she was still wearing, she advanced towards him. "Darling, *darling*! If only you'd said so before!" She held out her arms.

But instead of also saying "Darling!" and holding out *his* arms, the Savage backed away in terror, waving his hands at her as though he were trying to frighten away some dangerous animal. Four steps back, and he could move no further, his back against the wall.

"Sweet boy!" said Lenina, laying her hands on his shoulders and pressing herself against him. "Put your arms round me. Kiss me." She closed her eyes and let her voice sink into a sleepy whisper.

The Savage caught her by the wrists, tore her hands from his shoulders, and pushed her roughly away at arm's length.

"Ow, you're hurting me, you're . . . oh!" She was suddenly silent. Terror had made her forget the pain. Opening her eyes, she had seen his face — no, not *his* face, a crazy stranger's, pale, twisted, filled with some mad anger.

She tried to understand what had brought this madness into his face, but failed completely. "What is the matter, John?" she whispered. He did not answer, but only stared into her face with those mad eyes. The hands that held her wrists were trembling. He breathed deeply and unevenly. His lips curled back from his teeth. "What is the matter?" she almost screamed.

And as though woken by her cry he caught her by the shoulders and shook her. "Whore!" he shouted. "Whore from Hell!"

"Oh, don't, don't," she begged him in a voice which trembled from the shaking.

"Away with you!" He pushed her away with such force that she fell. "Go," he shouted, standing over her threateningly, "get out of my sight or I'll kill you."

Lenina raised her arm to cover her face. "No, please don't, John."

"Hurry up. Quick!"

One arm still raised, and following all his movements with a fearful eye, she struggled to her feet and, still covering her head, she rushed into the bathroom.

Outside, in the other room, the Savage marched up and down in anger. "Whore," he repeated to himself. "Disgusting whore."

"John," came a frightened voice from the bathroom, "do you think I might have my clothes?"

He picked up the pretty white blouse, the attractive sailor trousers.

"Open!" he ordered, kicking the door.

"No, I won't."

"Then how do you expect me to give them to you?"

"Push them through the little window over the door."

He did what she suggested, then went on marching up and down. Lenina sat listening to the footsteps in the other room, wondering, as she listened, how long he was likely to go on pacing up and down like that; whether she would have to wait until he left the flat; or if it would be safe, after allowing his madness a reasonable time to die down, to open the bathroom door and try to escape.

At that moment the telephone bell rang in the other room. She heard the voice of the Savage.

"Hullo."

. . . . . .

"Yes."

. . . . . .

"Yes, this is Mr Savage speaking."

. . . . . .

"What? Who's ill? Of course it interests me."

. . . . . .

"But is it serious? Is she really bad? I'll go at once . . ."

. . . . . .

"Not in her rooms any more? Where has she been taken?"

. . . . . .

"Oh, my God! What's the address?"

. . . . . .

"Three Park Lane — is that it? Three? Thanks."

Lenina heard the sound of the telephone being put back, then hurrying steps. A door shut loudly. There was silence. Had he really gone?

With great care she opened the door a quarter of an inch; looked through the crack, and, encouraged by the silence, put her head out; finally moved as quietly as she could into the room; stood for a few seconds with strongly beating heart, listening, listening; then rushed to the front door, opened, slipped through, banged it shut, ran. It was not till she was in the lift and actually going down that she began to feel safe.

Chapter 13

Death

The Park Lane Hospital for the Dying was a sixty-floor tower of bright yellow. As the Savage stepped out of his taxicopter, a line of brightly coloured funeral helicopters rose from the roof and went off across the Park, westwards, on their way to the Slough Crematorium. At the lift gates an official gave him the information he required, and he dropped down to the seventeenth floor. The ward where Linda was lying was a large room bright with sunshine and yellow paint, and contained twenty beds, all occupied. Linda was dying in company — in company and with all modern conveniences. The air was continuously alive with happy tunes coming from loudspeakers. At the foot of every bed, facing the dying person who occupied it, was a television set. Television was left on like a running water tap from morning till night.

"We try," said the nurse who met the Savage at the door, "to create a thoroughly pleasant atmosphere here — something between a first-class hotel and a cinema palace, if you take my meaning."

"Where is she?" asked the Savage, taking no notice of these polite explanations.

The nurse was offended. "You *are* in a hurry," she said.

"Is there any hope?" he asked.

"You mean, of her not dying?" (He nodded.) "No, of course there isn't. When somebody's sent here, there's no——" Alarmed by the look of worry on his pale face, she suddenly broke off. "Why, whatever is the matter?" she asked. She was not used to this kind of thing in visitors. (Not that there were many visitors anyhow; or any reason why there should be many visitors.) "You're not feeling ill, are you?"

He shook his head. "She's my mother," he said in a low voice.

The nurse gave him a look of horror, then quickly looked away, her face red and burning with discomfort.

"Take me to her," said the Savage, making an effort to speak in an ordinary tone.

Still very red, she led the way down the room. Linda was lying in the last of the long row of beds. Her eyes were closed. Her pale, swollen face wore a look of stupid happiness.

The nurse walked away. The Savage sat down beside the bed.

"Linda," he whispered, taking her hand.

At the sound of her name she turned. Her eyes opened. A look came into them as if she recognised him. She pressed his hand, she smiled, her lips moved; then quite suddenly her head fell forward. She was asleep. He sat watching her, remembering with tears in his eyes their life in the Reservation, especially all the stories she had told him about the Other Place, that beautiful, beautiful Other Place, whose memory, as of a heaven of goodness and loveliness, he kept fresh in his mind, unspoilt by contact with the disappointing reality of this real London, these actual civilised men and women.

His thoughts were interrupted by the arrival of a group of noisy child visitors, who had been brought by the Head Nurse to see the dying people as part of their conditioning, to get them used to death and dying people. He sent them away angrily from Linda's bedside, but when he sat down again his feelings and thoughts had changed. Instead of the gentle moments of his childhood, when Linda had been a kind and a loving mother to him, he could now remember only the ugly scenes of their life, with Popé in her bedroom and herself in an ugly sleep after drinking a great deal of *mescal*.

Linda moved, woke up and smiled, without understanding where she was.

"Popé," she whispered, and closing her eyes she sank back into the covers.

"But, Linda!" The Savage spoke anxiously. "Don't you know me?"

He pressed her hand again. "Don't you know me?"

He felt the faint answering pressure of her hand. The tears came into his eyes. He bent over her and kissed her.

Her lips moved. "Popé," she whispered again, and it was to him as though dirt had been thrown in his face. Anger suddenly boiled up in him — anger at the destruction of his hopes and ideals twice in so short a time, first by Lenina and now by his mother.

"But I'm John!" he shouted, "I'm John!" And in his extreme anger and unhappiness he actually caught her by the shoulder and shook her.

Linda's eyes opened again. She saw him, knew him.

"John!" she whispered. But it was as though she had forgotten how to breathe. A look of terror at his anger came into her eyes. Then her mouth fell open. Her breathing stopped. She was dead.

The Savage stared at her for a moment in frozen silence, then fell on his knees beside the bed and, covering his face with his hands, cried as though his heart would break.

The nurse stood in the middle of the ward, not knowing what to do. The child visitors were staring with wide eyes at this unpleasant scene. Should she speak to him? Try to bring him back to some attempt to behave properly? Remind him of where he was, of what harm he might do to these poor children, upsetting all their well-taught death-conditioning with this disgusting behaviour, as though death were something terrible, as though anyone mattered so much as all that.

She stepped forward, she touched him on the shoulder. "Can't you behave?" she said in a low, angry voice. But, looking round, she saw that several of the children were coming towards the bed. She must do something to turn their attention away from the Savage and his cries.

"Now, who wants a piece of chocolate?" she asked in a loud, cheerful voice.

"Me!" cried the entire Bokanovsky Group with one voice. The Savage and his grief were forgotten.

"Oh, God, God, God . . ." the Savage kept repeating to himself. In the river of sorrow that filled his mind it was the one word that he was able to say. "God!" he whispered it out loud. "God."

"Whatever is he saying?" said a voice, very near and distinct, through the sugary music which poured from the loudspeakers.

The Savage looked round sharply. Five light brown twins, each with the end of a stick of chocolate in his right hand and their faces dirty with chocolate, were standing in a row, all staring at him.

As he looked at them they all smiled. One of them pointed with his bit of chocolate.

"Is she dead?" he asked.

The Savage stared at them for a moment in silence. Then, in silence he rose to his feet, in silence slowly walked towards the door.

"Is she dead?" repeated the twin, running at his side, wanting to know.

The Savage looked down at him and still without speaking pushed him away. The twin fell on the floor and at once began to cry. The Savage did not even look round.

Chapter 14

Realities

The domestic staff of the Park Lane Hospital for the Dying consisted of one hundred and sixty-two Deltas divided into two Bokanovsky Groups of eighty-four red-headed female and seventy-eight dark-haired male twins. At six, when their working day was over, the two Groups gathered in the front hall of the Hospital and were served by a higher official with their *soma* tablets.

From the lift the Savage stepped out into the middle of them. But his mind was elsewhere with death, with grief, with his sadness. Without noticing what he was doing, he began to push his way through the crowd.

"Who are you pushing? Where do you think you're going?"

High, low, from a crowd of separate throats, only two voices came. Repeated countless times, as if by a mirror, two faces, one red-headed, the other dark-haired, turned angrily towards him. Their words and, in his chest, sharp digs from their elbows, brought him to his senses. He woke once more to the real world, looked round him, saw the endless crowd of similar beings around him. Twins, twins ... Twins had stared, smiling, at the dead Linda. Now, larger, fully-grown, they broke into his grief and his lost hope. He stopped and stared at the light brown crowd in the middle of which, taller than it by a full head, he stood. "O brave new world ..." he said sadly to himself.

"*Soma* distribution!" shouted a loud voice. "In good order. Hurry up there, please."

A door had been opened, a table and chair carried into the front hall. The voice was that of a cheerful young Alpha, who had entered carrying a black iron cash box. A low sound of satisfaction went up from the eager twins. They forgot all about the Savage. Their attention was now directed at the black cash box, which the young man had placed on the table and was now unlocking. The lid was lifted.

"Oh-oh!" said all the hundred and sixty-two voices in a single cry of joy.

The young man took out a handful of tiny boxes of tablets. "Now," he commanded, "step forward, please. One at a time and no shoving."

One at a time, with no shoving, the twins stepped forward. First two males, then a female, then another male, then three females, then ...

The Savage stood looking on. "O brave new world, O brave new world ..." In his mind the singing words seemed to change their tone.

They had laughed at him through his sadness and hopelessness. Now, suddenly, they rang out in a call to action. "O brave new world!" Miranda was telling of the possibility of loveliness, the possibility of changing even the life which surrounded him like a bad dream into something fine and noble. "O brave new world!" It was a challenge, a command.

"No shoving there, now!" shouted the official angrily. He shut his cash box noisily. "I shall stop the distribution unless I get good behaviour."

The Deltas pushed against one another a little, and then were still. His words had had their effect. Loss of *soma* — fearful thought!

"That's better," said the young man, and reopened his cash box.

Linda had been a slave, Linda had died. Others should live in freedom, and the world be made beautiful. And suddenly it was clear to the Savage what he must do.

"Now," said the official.

Another light brown female stepped forward.

"Stop!" called the Savage in a loud and ringing voice. "Stop!"

He pushed his way to the table. The Deltas stared at him with shock.

"Ford!" said the official below his breath. "It's the Savage!" He felt frightened.

"Listen, I beg you," cried the Savage, "Lend me your ears . . ."* He had never spoken in public before, and found it very difficult to express what he wanted to say. "Don't take that horrible stuff. It's poison, it's poison."

"I say, Mr Savage," said the official, with an uncertain smile, "would you mind letting me——"

"Poison to soul as well as body."

"Yes, but let me get on with my distribution, won't you? There's a good fellow." With the fear of one stroking an animal that might bite, he

*Lend me your ears: from Shakespeare's play *Julius Caesar*

touched the Savage's arm. "Just let me——"

"Never!" cried the Savage.

"But look here, old man——"

"Throw it all away, that horrible poison."

The words "Throw it all away" caught the attention of the stupid Deltas, made them realise what was happening. An angry cry went up from the crowd.

"I come to bring you freedom," said the Savage, turning back towards the twins, "I come——"

The official heard no more. He had slipped out of the hall and was looking for a number in the telephone book.

"Not in his own rooms," Bernard said. "Not in mine. Not at the Centre or the College. Where can he have got to?"

Helmholtz didn't know. They had come back from their work expecting to find the Savage waiting for them at one or other of their usual meeting places, and there was no sign of the fellow. This was upsetting their plans. They had meant to go over to Biarritz in Helmholtz's four-seater sporticopter. They'd be late for dinner if he didn't come soon.

"We'll give him five more minutes," said Helmholtz. If he doesn't turn up by then, we'll——"

The ringing of the telephone bell interrupted him. He picked up the receiver. "Hullo. Speaking." Then, after a long interval of listening, "Oh, Ford!" he cried. "I'll come at once."

"What is it?" Bernard asked.

"A fellow I know at the Park Lane Hospital," said Helmholtz. "The Savage is there. Seems to have gone mad. Anyhow, it's urgent. Will you come with me?"

Together they hurried along the corridor to the lifts.

"But do you like being slaves?" the Savage was saying as they entered the Hospital. His face was red, his eyes bright with passion and anger. "Do you like being babies? Yes, babies. Stupid babies all your lives?" he added, driven by their animal stupidity into throwing insults at those he had come to save. The insults fell off their thick skins; they stared at him with a blank expression in their eyes. "Yes, stupid!" he shouted. Grief and hopelessness, pity and duty, all were forgotten now and, as it were, melted into an uncontrollable hatred of these less than human beings. "Don't you want to be free men? Don't you even understand what it is to be a man and free? Don't you?" he repeated, but got no answer to his question. "Very well, then, I'll teach you. I'll *make* you free whether you want to or not." And pushing open the window that looked on to the inner court of the Hospital, he began to throw the little boxes of *soma* tablets out of it in handfuls.

For a moment the light brown crowd was silent, frozen with amazement and horror at the sight of this fearful crime.

"He's mad," whispered Bernard, staring with wide-open eyes. They'll kill him. They'll——"

A great shout suddenly went up from the crowd; a wave of movement drove it, threatening, towards the Savage. "Ford help him!" said Bernard, and turned his eyes away.

"Ford helps those who help themselves." And with a laugh, actually a laugh of joy, Helmholtz Watson pushed his way through the crowd.

"Free, free!" the Savage shouted, and with one hand continued to throw the *soma* into the courtyard while, with the other, he hit out at the indistinguishable faces of his attackers. "Free!" And suddenly there was Helmholtz at his side — "Good old Helmholtz!" — also hitting out. "Men at last!" Helmholtz cried and threw the poison out by handfuls through the open window. "Yes, men! men! men!" and there was no more poison left. He picked up the cash box and showed them its black emptiness. "You're free!"

Screaming with anger, the Deltas charged.

"They're done for," said Bernard and, with a sudden urge to help them, ran forward; then decided not to and stopped; then, ashamed, stepped forward again; then decided against it once more, and was standing there ashamed of his own fear — thinking that they might be killed if he didn't help them, and that he might be killed if he did — when (Ford be praised!) in ran the police, pig-faced in their gas masks.

Bernard rushed to meet them. He waved his arms; and it was action, he was doing something. He shouted "Help!" several times more and more loudly so as to persuade himself that he was helping. "Help! *Help!* HELP!"

The policemen pushed him out of the way and got on with their work. Three men with machines on their shoulders pumped thick clouds of *soma* gas into the air. Two more were busy with an Artificial Music Box. Carrying water guns loaded with a powerful sleeping gas, four others had pushed their way into the crowd and were steadily putting out of action the stronger of the fighters.

"Quick, quick!" screamed Bernard, "They'll be killed if you don't hurry. They'll . . . Oh!" Tired of his shouting, one of the policemen had given him a shot from his water gun. Bernard stood for a second or two on his shaky legs, then fell onto the floor.

Suddenly, from out of the Artificial Music Box, a Voice began to speak. The Voice of Reason, the Voice of Good Feeling. The soundtrack roll was unwinding itself in Artificial Crowd-Control Speech Number Two (Average Strength). Straight from the depths of a heart that had never existed, "My friends, my friends," said the Voice, with a note of such gentle sorrow that, behind their gas masks, even the policemen's eyes were for a moment filled with tears, "what is the meaning of this? Why aren't you all being happy and good together? Happy and good," the Voice repeated. It trembled, sank into a whisper and for a moment died away. "Oh, I do want you to be happy," it began again, "I do so want you to be good! Please, please be good and . . ."

Two minutes later the Voice and the *soma* gas had produced their effect. In tears, the Deltas were kissing and throwing their arms round one another; half a dozen twins held each other at a time. Even Helmholtz and the Savage were almost crying. A fresh supply of tablets was brought in from the Hospital stores; the *soma* was quickly given out and, to the sound of loving goodbyes from the Voice, the twins departed, crying as though their hearts would break. "Goodbye, my dearest, dearest friends, Ford keep you! Goodbye, my dearest, dearest friends, Ford keep you! Goodbye, my dearest, dearest . . ."

When the last of the Deltas had gone the policeman turned off the current. The heavenly Voice fell silent.

"Will you come quietly?" asked the Sergeant, "or must we put you to sleep?" He pointed his water gun.

"Oh, we'll come quietly," the Savage answered, wiping a cut lip and a bitten left hand.

Still keeping his hand to his bleeding nose, Helmholtz nodded in agreement.

Awake, and able to stand up again, Bernard had chosen this moment to move as quietly as he could towards the door.

"Hi, you there," called the Sergeant, and a gas-masked policeman hurried across the room and laid a hand on the young man's shoulder.

Bernard turned with an expression of surprise. Escaping? He hadn't dreamed of such a thing. "Though what on earth you want me for," he said to the Sergeant, "I really can't imagine."

"You're a friend of the prisoners, aren't you?"

"Well," said Bernard, and thought. No, he really couldn't deny it. "Why shouldn't I be?" he asked.

"Come on, then," said the Sergeant, and led the way towards the door and the waiting police car.

Chapter 15

In the Service of Happiness

The room into which the three were shown was the Controller's study.

"His fordship will be down in a moment." The Gamma manservant left them to themselves.

Helmholtz laughed out loud.

"It's more like a social gathering than a trial," he said, and let himself fall into the most comfortable of the armchairs.

"Cheer up, Bernard," he added, catching sight of his friend's pale, unhappy face. But Bernard would not be cheered. Without answering, without even looking at Helmholtz, he went and sat down on the most uncomfortable chair in the room, carefully chosen with some confused hope of turning away from him the anger of the higher powers.

The Savage meanwhile wandered restlessly round the room, looking without much interest at the books on the shelves, at the soundtrack rolls and the reading-machine films in their numbered places. On the table under the window lay a large volume bound in soft black artificial leather and stamped with large golden Ts. He picked it up and opened it. *My Life And Work*,* by Our Ford. The book had been published in Detroit by the Society for the Spread of Fordian Knowledge. He turned the pages slowly, read a sentence here, a paragraph there, and had just decided that the book didn't interest him, when the door opened and the World Controller for Western Europe walked quickly into the room.

Mustapha Mond shook hands with all three of them, but it was to the Savage that he addressed himself. "So you don't much like civilisation, Mr Savage," he said.

My Life and Work: a book by Henry Ford, written in 1922. In the New World this book becomes a holy book, taking the place of the Christian Bible.

The Savage looked at him. He had been prepared to lie, to argue, to remain rude and silent; but, encouraged by the good-humoured intelligence of the Controller's face, he decided to tell the truth, quite frankly. "No." He shook his head.

Bernard jumped and looked alarmed. What would the Controller think? To be identified as the friend of a man who said that he didn't like civilisation, said it openly and, of all people, to the Controller. It was terrible. "But, John," he began. A look from Mustapha Mond reduced him to a frightened silence.

"Of course," the Savage went on to admit, "there are some very nice things. All that music in the air, for instance . . ."

"Sometimes a thousand twangling instruments will hum about my ears, and sometimes voices."*

The Savage's face lit up with a sudden pleasure. "Have you read *The Tempest* too?" he asked. "I thought nobody knew about those plays here, in England."

"Almost nobody. I'm one of the very few. It's forbidden, you see. But as I make the laws here, I can also break them. Without being punished, Mr Marx," he added, turning to Bernard. "Which I'm afraid you *can't* do."

Bernard sank into a hopeless unhappiness.

"But why is it forbidden?" asked the Savage. In the excitement of meeting a man who had read Shakespeare he had for the moment forgotten everything else.

The Controller looked at him evenly. "Because it's old. That's the main reason. We haven't any use for old things here."

"Even when they're beautiful?"

"Particularly when they're beautiful. Beauty's attractive, and we don't

---

*Sometimes a thousand . . .: from Shakespeare's play *The Tempest*; "twangling" means making sounds produced by stringed instruments want people to be attracted by old things. We want them to like the new ones."

"But the new ones are so stupid and horrible. Those plays, where there's nothing but helicopters flying about and people kissing all the time." He made a face. "Goats and monkeys!" Only in Othello's words could he find satisfactory expression for his feelings of hatred.

"Nice animals, anyhow," said the Controller almost to himself.

"Why don't you let them see *Othello* instead?"

"I've told you. It's old. Besides, they couldn't understand it."

Yes. that was true. He remembered how Helmholtz had laughed at *Romeo and Juliet*. "Well, then," he said, after a pause, "something new that's like *Othello,* and that they could understand."

"That's what we've all been wanting to write," said Helmholtz, breaking a long silence.

"And it's what you never will write," said the Controller. "Because, if it were really like *Othello,* nobody could understand it, however new it might be. And if it were new, it couldn't possibly be like *Othello.*"

"Why not?"

"Yes, why not?" Helmholtz repeated. He too was forgetting the unpleasant realities of the situation. Only Bernard, pale with fear and anxiety about the future, remembered them. The others took no notice of him. "Why not?"

"Because our world is not Othello's world. You can't write sad stories where there is no unhappiness. The world's peaceful now. People are happy. They get what they want, and they never want what they can't get. They're well off. They're safe. They're never ill. They're not afraid of death. They know nothing of passion and old age. They don't have to worry about mothers and fathers. They've got no wives, or children, or loved ones to feel strongly about. They're so conditioned that they practically can't help behaving as they ought to behave. And if anything should go wrong, there's *soma*. Which you go and throw out of the window in the name of freedom, Mr Savage. *Freedom!*" He laughed. "Expecting Deltas to know what freedom is! And now expecting them to understand *Othello*! How can you have such an idea!"

The Savage was silent for a while. "All the same," he went on, sticking to his argument, "*Othello*'s good. *Othello*'s better than those films."

"Of course it is," the Controller agreed. "But that's the price we have to pay for stability. You've got to choose between happiness and what people used to call high art. We've given up the high art. We have the love films instead."

"But they don't mean anything."

"They mean themselves. They mean a lot of good feelings to the audience."

"But they're . . . they're written by stupid people."

The Controller laughed. "You're not being very polite to your friend Mr Watson. One of our most distinguished Emotional Engineers."

"But he's right," said Helmholtz, clearly upset. "Because it is stupid. Writing when there's nothing to say."

"Exactly. But that demands the greatest skill — making something out of practically nothing."

The Savage shook his head. "It all seems to me quite horrible."

"Of course it does. Happiness is never as exciting as unhappiness or the struggles of great passions. Happiness is never grand."

"I suppose not," said the Savage after a silence. "But need it be as bad as those twins?" He remembered all those long lines of ugly little twins waiting for their *soma*, smiling round Linda's deathbed, attacking him in a crowd with one face endlessly repeated. He looked at his bitten hand and trembled. "Horrible!"

"But how useful. I see you don't like our Bokanovsky Groups; but I assure you they're the foundation on which everything else is built. They provide the stability on which the whole social organisation depends."

"I was wondering," said the Savage, "why you had them at all, since you can get whatever you want out of those bottles. Why don't you make everybody an Alpha Double-Plus?"

Mustapha Mond laughed. "Because we have no wish to have our throats cut," he answered. "We believe in happiness and stability. A society of Alphas couldn't fail to be restless and unhappy. An Alpha would go mad if he had to do Epsilon work — or start destroying things. Only an Epsilon can be expected to make Epsilon sacrifices, for the good reason that for him they aren't sacrifices. His conditioning has determined the life he has got to live. He can't help himself."

The Savage was silent.

"The ideal population," said Mustapha Mond, "is like an iceberg — eight-ninths below the waterline, one-ninth above."

"And they're happy below the waterline?"

"Happier than above it. Happier than your friends here, for example." He pointed.

"In spite of that awful work?"

"Awful? *They* don't find it so. Quite the opposite, they like it. It's light, it's childishly simple. No strain on the mind or the muscles. Seven and a half hours of gentle labour, without too much bodily effort, and then the *soma* distribution and games and other amusements provided for them. What more can they ask for? True," he added, "they might ask for shorter hours, but would they be any the happier for that? No, they wouldn't. The experiment was tried, more than a century and a half ago. The whole of Ireland was put on to the four-hour day. What was the result? Unrest and a large increase in the amount of *soma* taken. The Inventions Office is full of plans for labour-saving processes. Thousands of them." Mustapha Mond waved his arms as if to give an idea of the great pile of plans. "And why don't we use them? For the sake of the workers. It would be cruelty to give them too much leisure. It's the same with agriculture. We could produce every mouthful of food artificially, if we wanted to. But we don't. We prefer to keep a third of the population on the land. For their own sakes, because it takes *longer* to get food out of the land than out of a factory. Besides, we have our stability to think of. We don't want to change. Every change is a threat to stability. That's another reason why we're so careful about using new inventions. Every discovery in pure science could lead to a revolution. Even science must sometimes be treated as a possible enemy. Yes, even science."

"What?" said Helmholtz in amazement, "But we're always teaching people that science is everything. That comes in sleep-teaching."

"Three times a week between seven and thirteen," added Bernard.

"And all the science propaganda we do at the College . . ."

"Yes, but what sort of science?" asked Mustapha Mond. "You've had no scientific training, so you can't judge. I was a pretty good scientist in my time. Too good — enough to realise that all our science is just a cookery book, with an official theory of cooking that nobody's allowed to question and a list of recipes that mustn't be added to except by special permission from the head cook. I'm the head cook now. But I was once a young kitchen boy with a taste for finding things out. I started doing a bit of cooking on my own. Unofficial cooking, unlawful cooking. A bit of real science, in fact." He was silent.

"What happened?" asked Helmholtz Watson.

The controller breathed deeply.

"Very nearly what's going to happen to you young men. I was on the point of being sent to an island."

Bernard started at these words. "Send me to an island?" He jumped up, ran across the room, and stood waving his arms in front of the Controller. "You can't send me. I haven't done anything. It was the others. I tell you it was the others." He pointed with an accusing finger to Helmholz and the Savage. "Oh, please don't send me to Iceland. I promise I'll do what I ought to do. Give me another chance. Please give me another chance." The tears began to fall. "I tell you it's their fault," he cried. "And not to Iceland. Oh, please, your fordship, please . . ." and in a fit of hopelessness he threw himself on his knees before the Controller. Mustapha Mond tried to make him get up, but he stayed there, crying and protesting.

In the end the Controller had to ring for his fourth secretary.

"Bring three men," he ordered, "and take Mr Marx into a bedroom. Give him some *soma* and then put him to bed and leave him."

The secretary went out and returned with three twin attendants in green uniforms. Still shouting and crying, Bernard was carried out.

"One would think he was going to have his throat cut," said the Controller, as the door closed. "If he had any sense, he'd realise that his punishment is really a reward. That's to say, he's being sent to a place where he'll meet the most interesting set of men and women to be found anywhere in the world. All the people who, for one reason or another, are too individual to fit into community life. All the people who aren't content to be the same as the others, who've got independent ideas of their own. Everyone, in a word, who's anyone. I almost wish it were me, Mr Watson."

Helmholtz laughed. "Then why aren't you on an island yourself?"

"Because, finally, I preferred this. I was given the choice; to be sent to an island, where I could have got on with my scientific work, or to be taken on to the Controller's Council with the certainty of myself becoming a Controller. I chose this and let the science go. I've gone on controlling ever since. It hasn't been very good for truth, of course. But it's been very good for happiness. Happiness has got to be paid for. You're paying for it, Mr Watson — paying because you happen to be too much interested in beauty. I was too much interested in truth. I paid too."

"But you didn't go to an island," said the Savage after a long silence.

The Controller smiled. "That's how I paid. By choosing to serve happiness. Other people's, not mine. It's lucky," he added, after a pause, "that there are such a lot of islands in the world. I don't know what we should do without them. Put you all in the gas chamber, I suppose. By the way, Mr Watson, would you like a tropical climate, or something that will keep you more lively?"

Helmholtz rose from his armchair. "I should like a thoroughly bad climate," he answered. "I believe one would write better if the climate were bad. If there were a lot of wind and storms, for example . . ."

The Controller nodded his approval. "I like your spirit, Mr Watson. I like it very much indeed. As much as I officially disapprove of it." He smiled. "What about the Falkland Islands?"

"Yes, I think that will do," Helmholtz answered. "And now, if you don't mind, I'll go and see how poor Bernard's getting on."

Chapter 16

The New God

"Art, science — you seem to have paid a fairly high price for your happiness," said the Savage when they were alone. "Anything else?"

"Well, religion, of course," replied the Controller. "At one time there used to be something called God. But I was forgetting: you know all about God, I suppose."

"Well . . ." The Savage paused. He would have liked to say something about being alone, about night, about the plain lying pale under the moon, about the fall into shadowy darkness, about death. He would have liked to speak, but there were no words. Not even in Shakespeare.

The Controller, meanwhile, had crossed to the other side of the room and was unlocking a large safe fixed into the wall between the bookshelves. The heavy door swung open. Feeling about in the darkness inside, "It's a subject," he said, "that has always had a great interest for me." He pulled out a thick black volume. "You've never read this, for example."

The Savage took it. "*The Holy Bible*," he read from the title page.

"Nor this." It was a small book and had lost its cover.

"*The Imitation of Christ*."

"Nor this." He picked out another one.

"*The Varieties of Religious Experience*. By William James."

"And I've got plenty more," Mustapha Mond continued, sitting down. "A whole collection of old, forbidden books. God in the safe and Ford on the shelves." He pointed with a laugh to his official library, to the shelves of books, the reading-machine films and soundtrack rolls.

"But if you know about God, why don't you tell them?" asked the Savage angrily. "Why don't you give them these books about God?"

"For the same reason as we don't give them *Othello*. They're old. They're about God hundreds of years ago. Not about God now."

"But God doesn't change."

"Men do, though."

"What difference does that make?"

"All the difference in the world. People used to turn to God when they were growing old and troubled and tired of the world. In the modern world we've got youth and happiness right up to the end. What follows? Evidently, that we can be independent of God. 'Religious feeling will make up to us all our losses', says the writer of one of these old books. But we haven't any losses to be made up. We don't need religious feeling."

"Then you think there is no God?"

"No, I think there quite probably is one."

"Then why——?"

Mustapha Mond cut him short. "But he shows himself in different ways to different men. In the old times he showed himself as the being that's described in these books. Now——"

"How does he show himself now?" asked the Savage.

"Well, he shows himself as if he weren't there at all. Where there is comfort there is no need for God."

"But I don't want comfort. I want God, I want poetry, I want real danger, I want freedom, I want goodness. I want sin."

"In fact," said Mustapha Mond, "you're claiming the right to be unhappy."

"All right, then," said the Savage, "I'm claiming the right to be unhappy."

"Not to mention the right to grow old and ugly and weak; the right to suffer disease; the right to have too little to eat; the right to live in constant fear of what may happen tomorrow; the right to fall a victim to pains of every kind."

There was a long silence.

"I claim them all," said the Savage at last.

Mustapha Mond spoke slowly. "You're welcome," he said.

Chapter 17

John Alone

The door was half open. They entered. "John!" From the bathroom came the unpleasant sound of somebody being violently sick.

"Is there anything the matter?" Helmholtz called.

There was no answer. The unpleasant sound was repeated, twice. There was silence. Then the bathroom door opened and, very pale, the Savage came out.

"I say," Helmholtz cried anxiously, "you *do* look ill, John."

"Did you eat something that upset you?" asked Bernard.

The Savage nodded. "I ate civilisation."

"What?"

"It poisoned me. And then," he added in a lower tone, "I ate my own evil nature."

"Yes, but what exactly . . . I mean, just now you . . ."

"Now I am pure again," said the Savage. "I drank some salty water."

The others stared at him in surprise. "Do you mean to say that you were doing it on purpose?" asked Bernard.

"That's how the Indians always make themselves pure." He sat down and wiped his forehead. "I shall rest for a few minutes," he said. "I'm rather tired."

"Well, I'm not surprised," said Helmholtz. After a silence, "We've come to say goodbye," he went on in another tone. "We're off tomorrow morning."

"Yes, we're off tomorrow," said Bernard, on whose face the Savage noticed a new expression of determined acceptance.

"And by the way, John," he continued, leaning forward in his chair and laying a hand on the Savage's knee, "I want to say how sorry I am about everything that happened yesterday." His face went red. "How ashamed," he went on, in spite of the trembling in his voice, "how really——"

The Savage cut him short and, taking his hand, pressed it in sympathy.

"Helmholtz was wonderful to me," Bernard went on, after a little pause. "If it hadn't been for him, I should——"

"Now, now," Helmholtz protested.

There was a silence. In spite of their sadness — because of it even, for their sadness was the sign of their love for one another — the three young men were happy.

"I went to see the Controller this morning," said the Savage at last.

"What for?"

"To ask if I could go to the islands with you."

"And what did he say?" asked Helmholtz eagerly.

The Savage shook his head. "He wouldn't let me."

"Why not?"

"He said he wanted to go on with the experiment. But I *won't*," said the Savage with sudden anger, "I won't go on being experimented with. Not for all the Controllers in the world. I shall go away tomorrow too."

"But where?" the others asked.

The Savage shook his head. "I don't know. Anywhere. I don't care. So long as I can be alone."

The helicopter airlane from London to Portsmouth was marked by a line of air-lighthouses which served to guide night-flyers. The line from Portsmouth to London ran roughly parallel to it, similarly marked, some distance to the west. At one point, in the county of Surrey, the old lines had been not more than six or seven kilometres apart. The distance was too small for careless flyers — particularly at night and when they had taken half a gram too much. There had been accidents. Serious ones. It had been decided to move the Portsmouth–London line a few kilometres further to the west. The course of the old line was marked by four deserted air-lighthouses. The skies above them were empty and silent.

The Savage had chosen for his lonely dwelling one of these lighthouses which stood on the top of a hill. The building was well-built and in good condition — almost too comfortable, the Savage had thought when he first looked round the place, almost too civilised. But he accepted it by promising himself that he would make his life all the harder, with the severest self-discipline. His first night there was passed without sleep. He spent the dark hours on his knees, praying to all the gods of whom he had heard in his childhood days in the Reservation. From time to time he stretched out his arms as though he were on the cross, and held them out until they ached. "Oh, forgive me," he prayed as the tears streamed down his face, "Oh, make me pure! Oh, help me to be good!" again and again, till he was on the point of fainting from the pain.

When morning came, he felt he had earned the right to live in the lighthouse, yes, even though there *was* still glass in most of the windows, even though the view from the platform *was* so fine. For the very reason for his choosing the lighthouse had become almost immediately a reason for going somewhere else. He had decided to live there because the view was so beautiful, because from that high place he seemed to be looking out on the loveliness of Heaven itself. But what right had he to be comforted with the daily and hourly sight of loveliness? All he deserved to live in was some blind hole in the ground. Stiff and still aching after his long night of pain, but feeling comforted because of it, he climbed to the platform of his tower, he looked out over the bright, sunlit land. To the north the view ended with the long line of hills known as the Hog's Back. In the valley which separated these hills from the sandy hill on which the lighthouse stood, there was a little village with a chicken farm, only nine floors high. On the other side of the lighthouse, towards the south, the ground fell away in long slopes of rough grass and low bushes to a chain of small lakes.

It was this slope that had attracted the Savage to the lighthouse. The woods, the open stretches of yellow-flowering bushes, the tall trees, the shining lakes — these were beautiful and, to an eye used to the dry wastes of the American desert, amazing. And then the quietness! Whole days passed during which he never saw a human being. The lighthouse was only a quarter of an hour's flight from the Charing-T Tower, but the hills of Malpais were hardly more empty than this little spot. The crowds that left London daily left it only to play Obstacle Golf or Tennis. There were no golf clubs in the area. The nearest artificial tennis courts were several miles away. Flowers and scenery were the only attractions here. And so, as there was no good reason for coming, nobody came. During the first few days the Savage lived alone and in peace.

Of the money which, on his first arrival, John had received for his personal expenses, most had been spent on equipment that he needed for his new life. He counted his money. The little that remained, he hoped, would be enough to last him through the winter. By next spring, his garden would be producing enough to make him independent of the outside world. Meanwhile, there would always be wild animals. He had seen plenty of rabbits, and there were wild duck on the lakes. He set to work at once to make a bow and arrows.

There were young trees, beautifully straight, in a little wood near the lighthouse. He began by cutting down one which gave him six feet of straight stem without branches. He took off the outer covering of the tree and then gradually and very carefully cut away the white wood, as old Mitsima had taught him, until he had a strong stick, of his own height, stiff at the centre where it was thickest, lively as a steel spring at the tips. After those weeks in London, with nothing to do, whenever he wanted anything, but to press a switch or turn a handle, it was pure joy to be doing something that demanded skill and patience.

He had almost finished shaping the staff when he realised with a shock that he was singing — *singing*! He stopped, feeling very guilty. After all, it was not to sing and enjoy himself that he had come here. It was to escape from the disgusting contact with civilised life. It was to be made pure and good. He realised that he had forgotten what he had promised to himself that he would remember — poor Linda and his own murderous unkindness to her in her last moments. He had come here to show how deep was his sorrow. And here he was, sitting happily making his bow, singing, actually singing . . .

He went inside, opened the box of salt, and put some water on to boil.

Half an hour later, three Delta-Minus land workers who happened to be driving past were shocked to see a young man standing beside the abandoned lighthouse naked to the waist and hitting himself with a knotted whip. His back was marked with thin red lines, and between them ran drops of blood. The driver of the lorry stopped at the side of the road and, with his two friends, stared open-mouthed at the extraordinary sight. One, two, three — they counted the strokes. After the eighth, the young man interrupted his self-punishment to run to the wood's edge and there be violently sick. When he had finished, he picked up the whip and began hitting himself again — nine, ten, eleven, twelve . . .

"Ford!" whispered the driver. And his twins were of the same opinion.

"Fordey!" they said.

Three days later, like birds settling on a dead body, the reporters came.

Dried and hardened over a slow fire of green wood, the bow was ready. The Savage was busy on his arrows. Thirty straight sticks had been dried, tipped with sharp nails, and a V-shaped cut carefully made at the other end of each one, where the string would fit. He had secretly visited the chicken farm one night, and now had enough feathers for all his needs. He was putting feathers on one of his arrows when the first of the reporters arrived. Noiseless on rubber shoes, the man came up behind him.

"Good morning, Mr Savage," he said. "I am the representative of *The Hourly Radio*."

Taken by surprise, the Savage sprang to his feet as if a snake had bitten him, scattering arrows and feathers in all directions.

"I beg your pardon," said the reporter. "I'm sorry."

He touched his hat — a tall hat of light metal in which he carried his radio equipment. "Excuse my not taking it off," he said. "It's a bit heavy. Well, as I was saying. I am the representative of *The Hourly*——"

"What do you want?" asked the Savage angrily.

The reporter smiled his most friendly smile.

"Well, of course, our readers would be very interested in a few words from you, Mr Savage." He smiled more pleasantly than ever, "Just a few words from you, Mr Savage." And in a very few moments he had taken wires from his pocket, connected them to his radio set and turned it on. "Hullo," he said into a microphone which the touch of a spring had caused to hang down from his hat and in front of his mouth. A bell suddenly rang inside his hat. "Is that you, Edzel? Primo Mellon speaking. Yes, I've managed to find him. He's here. Mr Savage will now take the microphone and say a few words. Won't you, Mr Savage?" He looked up at the Savage with another of those winning smiles. "Just tell our readers why you came here. What made you leave London (hold on, Edzel) so suddenly. And, of course, that whip. (The Savage jumped. How did they know about the whip?) And then something about Civilisation. You know the sort of stuff. 'What I think of the Civilised Girl.' Just a few words, a very few . . ."

The Savage obeyed, but not in the way Mr Mellon expected. Two words he spoke, no more, and then repeated them. "Get out!" he shouted, "Get out!" And seizing the reporter by the shoulder he spun him round and, with all the force and skill of a champion football player, kicked him violently on his well-covered bottom.

Eight minutes later, a new edition of *The Hourly Radio* was on sale in the streets of London. "HOURLY RADIO REPORTER KICKED BY MYSTERY SAVAGE" said the headline on the front page.

In spite of what Mellon had suffered, four other reporters called that afternoon at the lighthouse. Each one was received more violently than the one before.

From a safe distance and still rubbing the sore place where the kick had landed, one of them shouted, "You madman, why don't you take *soma*? That would make you feel better."

"Oh, would it?" said the Savage, picking up a large stick and moving towards him. The reporter made a rush for his helicopter.

The Savage was left for a time in peace. A few helicopters came and circled the tower. He shot an arrow into the nearest of them. It went through the light metal floor of the helicopter. There was a cry of pain, and the machine shot up into the air with all the speed and power that its engines could give it. After that the others kept their distance respectfully. Taking no further notice of them, the Savage dug at what was to be his garden. After a time they grew tired of waiting, since nothing seemed to be happening, and flew away.

The weather was very hot, there was thunder in the air. He had dug all the morning and was resting, stretched out along the floor. And suddenly Lenina came into his thoughts, as real as if she were there in the lighthouse with him, naked, saying "Darling!" and "Put your arms round me!" — in shoes and socks and smelling sweet. Shameless woman! But oh, oh, her arms round his neck, her soft red lips, her smooth white skin! Lenina . . . No, no, no, no! He sprang to his feet and ran out of the house. At the edge of the wood there stood an old bush with needle-like leaves. He threw himself against it, he held closely not the smooth body of his desires, but an armful of sharp green points. They gave him great pain. He tried to think of poor Linda, breathless, silent, with terror in her eyes. Poor Linda, whom he had promised to remember. But it was still the presence of Lenina that filled his mind. Lenina, whom he had promised to forget. Even through the sting of the bush he could feel her, unavoidably real. "Sweet, sweet . . . And if you wanted me too, why didn't you . . ."

The whip was hanging on a nail by the door, ready for use should any more reporters arrive. In anger the Savage ran back to the house, seized it, swung it in the air. The knots bit into his flesh.

"Whore, whore!" he shouted at every blow as though it were Lenina (and how greatly, without knowing it, he wished it were!), white, warm, sweet-smelling, shameless Lenina that he was whipping thus. "Shameless!" And then, desperately, "Oh, Linda, forgive me. Forgive me, God! I'm bad! I'm evil! I'm . . . No, no, you whore, you whore!"

From his carefully built hiding place in the wood three hundred metres away, Darwin Bonaparte, the Television Corporation's most expert big-game photographer, had watched the whole scene. Patience and skill had been rewarded. He had spent three days sitting inside the trunk of an artificial tree, three nights moving around on his stomach through the long grass, hiding equipment in bushes, burying wires in the soft grey sand. Seventy-two hours of the greatest discomfort. But now the great moment had come — the greatest, thought Darwin Bonaparte, as he moved among his equipment, the greatest since his exciting film of the monkeys' wedding. "Wonderful," he said to himself, as the Savage began his amazing performance, "Wonderful!" He kept his long-distance cameras carefully aimed at the Savage; (adjusted the settings) to get a close-up of the face, twisted with anger and pain (admirable!); changed for half a minute to slow motion (a really amusing effect, he promised himself); listened meanwhile to the blows, the cries, the wild and mad words that were being recorded on the soundtrack at the edge of his film; was very happy to hear, in a quiet moment, the singing of a wild bird; wished the Savage would turn round so that he could get a good close-up of the blood on his back — and almost immediately (what amazing luck!) the Savage did turn round, and he was able to take a perfect close-up.

"Well, that was great," he said to himself when it was all over. "Really great!" He wiped his face with a cloth. When they had finished with it at the studio, it would be a wonderful film.

Twelve days later *The Savage of Surrey* was being shown in every first-class cinema in Western Europe.

The effect of Darwin Bonaparte's film was immediate and enormous. On the afternoon which followed the evening of its first performance, the peace of John's lonely home was suddenly broken by the arrival overhead of a great cloud of helicopters. He was digging in his garden — digging, too, in his own mind, thinking of Death. Death. And he drove in his spade once, and again, and yet again. "And all our yesterdays have lighted fools the way to dusty death."* He lifted another spadeful of earth. Why had Linda died? Why had she been allowed to become gradually less than human and at last . . . he trembled.

At that point the sky grew dark. He was suddenly in shadow. There was something between the sun and him. He looked up in surprise from his digging, from his thoughts, and saw, close above him, the cloud of machines, hanging in the air. They came like harmful insects, stopped in the air over his head for a moment, then dropped all around him in the long grass and among the bushes. And from the bodies of these huge insects stepped men in white artificial woollen trousers, women in artificial cotton shorts and artificial silk shirts, one couple from each. In a few minutes there were dozens of them, standing in a wide circle round the lighthouse, staring, taking photographs, throwing nuts and sweets as if at an animal in a zoo. And every moment, coming in from all sides in a never-ending stream, their numbers grew and grew.

The Savage had gone back into his house and now, like an animal trapped by the hunters, stood with his back to the wall of the lighthouse, staring from face to face in speechless horror, like a man out of his senses.

"Go away!" he shouted.

The animal had spoken. The crowd laughed and waved their hands. "Good old Savage! Hurrah, hurrah!" And through the noise he heard cries of "Whip, whip, the whip!"

The word stung him to action. He seized the knotted whip from its nail behind the door and shook it at them.

They shook with laughter.

He advanced towards them, a terrible figure. A woman cried out in fear. The line of people moved back a little, then stood firm. The thought that they were there in great numbers gave them a courage which the Savage had not expected.

"Why don't you leave me alone?" There was a suggestion of tears in

*And all our yesterdays . . .: from Shakespeare's play *Macbeth*

his anger. "What do you want with me?" he asked, turning from one stupid, smiling face to another.

"The whip," answered a hundred voices in one shout. "Let's see you do the whipping act."

Then altogether, slowly and heavily, "We — want — the whip," shouted a group at the end of the line. "We — want — the whip."

Others at once took up the cry, and the phrase was repeated again and again, more and more loudly, until no other word was being spoken. "We — want — the whip."

At this moment yet another helicopter arrived. When it landed, the door opened and out stepped, first a red-faced young man, then, in green artificial cotton shorts, white shirt and smart cap, a young woman.

At the sight of the young woman the Savage turned pale and fell back.

The young woman stood, smiling at him, an uncertain smile, a smile intended to calm him. The seconds passed. Her lips moved. She was saying something; but the sound of her voice was drowned by the shouts of the crowd.

"We — want — the whip! We — want — the whip!"

The young woman pressed both hands to her left side, and on that face of hers with its childlike prettiness appeared an unusual expression of sadness. Her blue eyes seemed to grow larger, brighter; and suddenly two tears rolled down her cheeks. Her mouth moved again, though her words could not be heard. Then, with a quick movement of passion, she stretched out her arms towards the Savage and stepped forward.

"We — want — the whip! We want —— "

And all of a sudden they had what they wanted.

"Shameless!" The Savage had rushed at her like a madman, striking her violently with his whip.

She had turned to run from him in terror, had caught her foot in the roots of the bushes and had fallen on her face in the long grass. "Henry, Henry!" she shouted. But her red-faced friend had run away and hidden behind the helicopter.

The crowd rushed towards the spot where the Savage stood, striking at that soft body lying in the grass.

"Oh, the flesh, the flesh!" This time it was on the Savage's own shoulders that the whip came down.

Drawn by the strange attraction of the horror of pain, and driven on by that desire to act as all others acted, that their conditioning had rooted in them, they began to imitate his violent action, striking at one another as the Savage struck at his own flesh or at that shapely, shameless body twisting and turning in pain in the grass at his feet.

"Kill it, kill it, kill it . . ." the Savage went on shouting.

Then suddenly somebody started "Orgy-porgy", and in a moment they had all caught up the tune and, singing, had begun to dance. Orgy-porgy, round and round and round, beating one another in time to the song. Orgy-porgy . . .

It was after midnight when the last of the helicopters took its flight. Stupid with *soma*, and tired out from endless uncontrolled hours of passion, the Savage lay sleeping in the rough grass. The sun was already high when he woke. He lay for a moment, then suddenly remembered everything.

"Oh, my God, my God!" He covered his eyes with his hand.

That evening the sky was black with helicopters making their way across the sky to the lighthouse in an endless stream. The description of last night's events had been in all the papers.

"Savage!" called the first arrivals, as they stepped down from their machine. "Mr Savage!"

There was no answer.

The door of the lighthouse stood half open. They pushed it wide open and walked into the low light inside. Through a doorway on the other side of the room they could see the bottom of the stairs that led up to the higher floors. Just under the top of the doorway hung a pair of feet. "Mr Savage!"

Slowly, very slowly, like two unhurried compass needles, the feet turned towards the right; north, north-east, east, south-east, south, south-south-west; then paused, and, after a few seconds, turned as unhurriedly back towards the left. South-south-west, south, south-east, east . . .

Word List

arrow (n) a weapon like a thin straight stick with a point at the end that you shoot from a **bow**

balloon (n) a large bag of strong light cloth filled with gas that can float in the air

bow (n) a weapon used for shooting **arrows** made from a long thin curved piece of wood with a string tied between the ends

compass (n) a piece of equipment with a needle that shows direction

crematorium (n) a building in which dead bodies are burned

contraceptive (n) a drug, object or method that makes it possible for a woman to have sex without having a baby

embryo (n) an animal or human that has not yet been born, and is in its first stage of development

eyebrow (n) the line of hair above your eye

fertilise (v) to make a male seed join with a female egg so that an **embryo** is created

hatch (v) to cause a creature to be born from an egg

helicopter (n) a type of aircraft with large metal blades on top which spin very quickly to make it fly

hum (n/v) a low continuous sound like the sound of heavy traffic in the distance

iceberg (n) a very large mass of ice floating in the sea, most of which is under water

imitate (v) to copy something or somebody

mask (n) something that covers all or part of your face, to protect or hide it

mescal (n) a very strong alcoholic Mexican drink

motto (n) a short statement which expresses the aims or beliefs of a person or organisation

naked (adj) not wearing clothes

obstacle (n) an object that is in your way so that you must try to get around it

passion (n) very strong, deeply felt emotion

phosphorus (n) a chemical that is useful in farming

propaganda (n) information, often false, used by governments to make people agree with them

recipe (n) a set of instructions for cooking a particular type of food

rocket (n) a vehicle used for travelling in space, shaped like a tube

sacrifice (n/v) an animal or person that is killed in a ceremony and offered to a god; to do without something you want in order to get something more important

savage (n/adj) an old-fashioned and insulting word for someone from a place where the way of living seems simple and underdeveloped; very cruel and violent

soma (n) an Indian drug that makes people forget their troubles and be happy

sterilise (v) to perform an operation that makes a person or animal unable to have babies

twin (n) one of two children who are born at the same time and look the same if they come from the same egg

whore (n) an insulting word for a woman who has sex for money

Activities

Chapters 1–3

Before you read

1   Look at these sentences from Chapter 1. The Director of the Central London
     Hatching and Conditioning Centre is explaining the work of the Centre to a
     group of students:
     "One egg, one embryo, one adult — that is normal. But a bokanovskified egg
     will divide into many others — from eight to ninety-six — and every one will
     grow into a perfectly formed embryo, and every embryo into a full-sized
     adult. Producing ninety-six human beings instead of one. Progress."
     What does this tell you about the way that babies are produced in this future
     society? Why do you think they are produced in this way?

After you read: Understanding

2   Name the five main types of baby produced in the Centre. Which is the most
     intelligent?

3   What happens in:
     1   the Bottling Room?
     2   the Organ Store?
     3   the Nursery bedrooms?

4   What is the purpose of:
     1   Bokanovsky's Process?
     2   sleep-teaching?
     3   a Malthusian belt?

After you read: Speaking

5   Explain how and why the Centre conditions Delta infants to be afraid of
     flowers and books.

6   Explain why Fanny disapproves of Lenina's relationship with Henry Foster and why she is surprised about Lenina's interest in Bernard Marx. What does their conversation tell us about sexual morality in this future world?

Chapters 4–6

Before you read

7   What do you think Lenina is going to do next? What will the outcome be?

After you read: Understanding

8   Name:
1   two forms of air transport mentioned in the story.
2   a popular sport.
3   the highest building in the city.
4   the place where dead bodies are taken.
5   the god-figure in this society.

9   Read this sentence from Chapter 4:
"Too much intelligence had produced in Helmholtz Watson effects very like those which, in Bernard Marx, were the result of a body not sufficiently developed."
What exactly are these "effects"?

After you read: Speaking

10   Discuss Bernard's feelings at various points in these chapters. To what extent are these feelings normal in this society?
1   How does he feel about Lenina before he knows her?
2   How does he feel after the Unity Service?
3   How does he feel after he and Lenina have slept together?
4   How does he feel after the Director of Hatching and Conditioning has warned him about his failure to submit to the rules for social behaviour?

Chapters 7–9

Before you read

11   What do you expect life to be like in the Reservation? How do you think
     Lenina and Bernard will react to life there?

After you read: Understanding

12   Complete these sentences.
     1   John's mother is called ....
     2   John was born in ....
     3   His mother used to live in ....
     4   She came to Malpais with ....
     5   Popé brought a book for John called ....
     6   Bernard decides to take John to ....

13   Are these sentences true or false?
     1   Linda is the Director of Hatching and Conditioning's wife.
     2   The Director is John's father.
     3   John looks like other savages.
     4   The Director does not approve of Bernard.
     5   The Director's past is the cause of amusement to his staff.
     6   Bernard is sent to Iceland.

After you read: Speaking

14   Imagine you are Lenina. Describe to your friend Fanny what happened in the
     village square.

15   Discuss the differences between life in the New World and life in Malpais.

16   Work in groups of three. Take the roles of the Director, Bernard and Linda,
     and act out the scene in the Fertilising Room when Linda meets the Director
     again.

Chapters 10–13

Before you read

17 How do you think Linda and John will respond to living in the New World? What features of it will they enjoy? What will shock them?

After you read: Understanding

18 Answer these questions.
1 Why is Linda of no interest to the "best people"?
2 How does Linda spend her time?
3 How does Bernard's social life change?
4 Who goes to the cinema with John?
5 How does John feel about Lenina?
6 How does Lenina feel about John?
7 What leads to Linda's death?

After you read: Speaking

19 Discuss how the scene around Linda's deathbed shows the differences in attitude between John and the people of the New World. Which attitude do you think is healthier for individuals and for society generally?

Chapters 14–17

Before you read

20 In Chapter 14, John stops the hospital domestic staff from taking their *soma* by throwing it out of the window. What do you think will happen as a result of his action?

After you read: Understanding

21 Who is speaking to whom? What are they talking about?
1 "I come to bring you freedom."
2 "Oh Ford! . . . I'll come at once."
3 " . . . must we put you to sleep?"

4   "The ideal population . . . is like an iceberg — eight-ninths below the waterline, one-ninth above."

5   "But if you know about God, why don't you tell them?"

6   "Oh, Linda, forgive me. Forgive me, God! I'm bad! I'm evil!"

7   "We — want — the whip! We — want — the whip!"

After you read: Speaking

22   Explain why Mustapha Mond feels that:
1   Shakespeare's plays need to be banned.
2   you can't have a society in which everyone is an intellectual.
3   labour-saving machines are not always helpful to society.
4   there is no need for God in the New World.

Whole book

Writing

1   Did you find the book interesting? Give your reasons.

2   Imagine you are Bernard and you are in Malpais. Write a letter to your friend Helmholtz describing some aspects of life there that you think he will find interesting.

3   Describe how Lenina changes during the story.

4   Imagine a different ending to the story. Write what could have happened.

5   Do you think that people in our own world are conditioned to do certain things? Justify your arguments, giving specific examples.

6   Do you agree with Mustapha Mond that happiness and social stability are more important than individual freedom? Argue your case.